THE SECRET SANTA MYSTERY

The Highland Horse Whisperer Mysteries Prequel

R.B. MARSHALL

Find out more about the author and upcoming books online at rozmarshall. co.uk/books

Get **your FREE starter library**—sign up for my newsletter: rozmarshall. co.uk/newsletter

ON LANGUAGE AND SPELLING

A NOTE TO MY AMERICAN READERS:

The characters in this book are British, and the heroine is Scottish, so it would seem strange if they spoke American English.

Because of that, the British spelling and grammar used here might appear like spelling errors.

For example: realise (British spelling), realize (American spelling); colour (British), color (American); panelled / paneled; dialogue / dialog and so on.

We also use some words differently (eg our leg wear is trousers, not pants) and have some colourful dialect phrases ('brass neck', 'lose the rag') so I've included a **Glossary** at the back which I hope will be helpful.

ABOUT THIS BOOK

A SECRET SANTA—WITH A SECRET!

Security expert for a British bank by day, horse trainer at night, Izzy Paterson is a multi-tasking, dressage-riding, computer whiz with an addiction to strong coffee and a penchant for CSI on Netflix. So when she's handed a perplexing riddle by the Secret Santa at her office Christmas party, she just can't ignore the mystery.

Penned by a modern-day Robin Hood, the anonymous rhyme hints at financial misconduct that could put the future of everyone at her work in danger.

Despite herself, Izzy is drawn into solving the puzzle, delving into the furthest reaches of the internet in her quest to track down the mysterious wrongdoer. Can she solve the mystery before the company implodes, or before her adversary takes things from the virtual to the physical—and still get home to Scotland in time for Christmas?

THE SECRET SANTA MYSTERY

CHAPTER ONE

A BONY ELBOW poked me in the ribs. "Izzy!" hissed my
colleague Devlin Connolly, known to his friends as Dev.
"Who did you buy for this year?"

"It wouldn't be a *secret* Santa if I told you, would it?"

He gave me what he thought was an innocent look. On a
six-foot Irishman with wild black hair and two days worth of
stubble, it had more in common with sinister than with
sinless. "But you can tell me, sure you can. I can absolutely
keep a secret."

I skewered him with some prime side-eye. "Suffice to say I
didn't buy for you. Although you'd have been a lot easier to
shop for than my *real* target. I could just have got you a cater-
ing-size box of Skittles."

Shoulders hunching, he had the grace to look shameful.
"At least they're not addictive."

My eyebrows climbed towards my hairline.

"I could give them up anytime," Dev said, sliding an arm
behind his back. I felt sure he was crossing his fingers.

In honour of the occasion, he'd ditched his usual outfit of

superhero t-shirt and jeans, and was wearing beige chinos and a blue-checked shirt. He almost looked smart, for a change.

"Maybe that should be your New Year's Resolution." I grinned at him. "No more snacking on sweeties while sat at your desk."

"There's at least three weeks till—"

At the front of the room, Gordon Dempsey, our CEO, stepped ponderously to the microphone. "Colleagues!" he cried, interrupting Dev, and looking out at us in the slightly unfocussed way of someone who has overindulged at the free bar.

Despite having the money to dress in Armani, Mr Dempsey had this uncanny knack of making even designer clothes look shabby. With his tie hanging at half mast and the silver buttons on his waistcoat struggling to contain his ample girth, he was not the ideal poster-boy for our organisation.

"Uh-oh," I said, nudging Dev. "Dempo is about to speechify."

Dev rolled his eyes. "Pity save us."

The other six people at our table were also IT staff from Bleubank, one of the major financial institutions in the City of London. But Dev was the one I knew best, and the only one I'd call a friend.

Across from us sat Manda Kumar, the third—and quietest —member of our team. We'd worked together for over a year, but I knew very little about her, apart from the fact that she liked to read celebrity gossip magazines, and had an over-bearing mother who phoned, without fail, every lunchtime.

Four other seats were taken up with staff from the web and server section, and at the head of the table sat our team leader, Nicholas Spence. Thin face scowling and pale skin flushed, his thumbs jabbed like knives at the keyboard on his phone.

An exaggerated throat-clearing drew our attention back

to the front. Mr Dempsey's pudgy lips curled into something approximating to a smile as he stepped closer to the microphone. "It's that time again. Time for Bleubank employees to show their ingenuity—and generosity," he added, with all the aplomb of an old-fashioned music hall master of ceremonies. "What goodies will Santa have for you this year?" With a flourish, he pointed to the side of the hall.

Our office Christmas lunch was being held in a restored corn exchange not far from the Tower of London. Oak-panelled walls soared to a beamed ceiling, and in a corner stood a towering evergreen adorned with red baubles and silver tinsel. The faint aroma of fresh pine needles reached us even at our table near the back.

Right on cue, a hidden door beside the tree opened to reveal a fat figure clothed in red and white, carrying a bulging sack. More North Pimlico than North Pole, Santa's tunic strained over a belly that was probably a result of too many business lunches. Not only that, but the red nose that peeked from under suspiciously white eyebrows looked like it owed more to malt whisky than mince pies.

The CEO ostentatiously delved into Santa's sack, pulled out a gift, and called the first name. "Iris Hooper! Come on down!"

A small, mouse-like woman, our CFO's secretary, scurried from her seat two tables away, and almost curtsied before the unidentified manager who'd dressed up as Father Christmas. He handed her a pink-wrapped present and leaned forward for a kiss before she could avoid him.

Dev got called up before I did and came back to the table clutching a gift bag decorated with frolicking penguins. Pulling the handles apart, he peered inside, then looked accusingly at me. "Why would you be lying to me?"

My forehead scrunched quizzically.

"Look!" He thrust the bag in my direction.

It was filled almost to the brim with rainbow-hued packets of Skittles.

I was still laughing at him when my name was finally called a minute later. Wiping quickly under my eyes with a tissue, I headed to the front of the room, suddenly feeling self-conscious.

Why was it I could confidently ride into a competition arena in front of ranks of spectators when sat on Leo, my dressage horse? But ask me to walk a few steps in front of my work colleagues and I'd be stumbling and tripping like I had two left feet.

It wasn't like I'd been drinking. Unlike pretty much everyone else here, I had work to do afterwards. Or perhaps that should be sport to do afterwards...

Murphy's Law dictated that the Friday two-and-a-half weeks before the world celebrated Jesus' birthday would not only be my work's festive do, but also the day of the Christmas party for the staff at the livery stables where I kept Leo. Which meant that I had to travel there after work, change my fancy clothes for jeans and leather boots, and clean out his box.

And sobriety was definitely recommended when negotiating a stinking muck heap with a dodgy wheelbarrow. Plus, I had a busy weekend coming up with a long drive on Saturday, so I needed all my wits about me.

Pulling myself together, I tried to channel confident horsewoman rather than introverted computer geek, and strode forward.

When I finally reached the surrogate Santa, he handed me a somewhat inauspicious envelope, then puckered up and leaned in. "Not tonight, buddy," I muttered under my breath, and deftly turned my head so his lips met my cheek.

Buoyed by this small victory, I was back in my seat before I'd had time to become embarrassed again.

"So what did you get?" Dev demanded.

I held out the envelope. "Just this."

"Open it, then."

Working with horses on a regular basis meant that I had no nails to speak of, so I plucked a clean knife from Manda's side plate, and sliced the packet open.

Inside was a voucher for a horse tack and feed shop in Richmond, near the livery stables. Obviously my Secret Santa knew at least *something* about me. I waved it at Dev. "I can get some treats for Leo." I glimpsed my nails again. "Or gloves for me."

The card that accompanied the gift had a quaint picture of a mare and foal on the front. But it was the inscription inside that caught my eye and piqued my interest. They had printed it on white paper, cut it out, then stuck it onto the card:

> *If mystery is your game*
> *And honesty your aim*
> *In dark places you should seek*
> *The Secret you must keep*
>
> *From foreign places go*
> *And track both high and low*
> *Try following the money*
> *For clues will reveal the honey*
>
> *Your route may lead to failure*
> *And perils will assail you*
> *But truth will always win*
> *When bravery comes in*
> Robin Hood 1454

Sitting back in my chair, I puffed out a breath. *Robin Hood.*

But the verse said nothing about his merry men or the sheriff of Nottingham. What could it mean?

I was about to show it to Dev, when the phrase *'The Secret you must keep'* jumped out at me. *Perhaps I'll just keep it to myself for now,* I thought. I slid the card back into the envelope, which was plain white and had my name written on the front in block capitals.

That was the only personalised thing about the gift, other than the fact that the giver knew I liked horses. But anyone that passed my desk at work would know that, since I used a picture of Leo as a screensaver and had a dressage calendar pinned to the partition beside me.

At the front of the room, Santa handed out the final present, then Mr Dempsey clapped his hands. "Last orders at the bar, ladies and gentlemen." He pulled a device from his pocket and checked the screen. "We have the place for another twenty minutes." With a flourish like a demented magician, he pressed a button on the gadget. Irritating Christmas musak streamed from loudspeakers high on the walls, grating at my eardrums.

I took that as my cue to leave. It's not that I don't like Christmas. I enjoy being with my family in Scotland on Christmas Day as much as the next person. But the enforced jollity and tinsel-wrapped commercialisation that begins before autumn has properly ended just annoys me. Somehow, the festive period has become a retail juggernaut, and the real reason for the season has been lost.

Stuffing the gift voucher, envelope and card into my black messenger bag, I slid out of my seat. "See you on Monday," I said to Dev, and waved my fingers at the rest of the table. "Catch you later."

A minute afterward I stepped onto the busy street outside the corn exchange and hugged my jacket around me. There was a nip in the air, although in crowded London it seldom got cold enough for frost. I wrinkled my nose. The faint breeze smelled of overflowing bins and car exhaust. *Lovely.* If it wasn't for my work, I'd live as far away from London as possible.

Born in a small town on the outskirts of Edinburgh, I'd gone to school there, studied Computer Science at Glasgow University, then done a Master's degree at Dundee University. But it turned out that all the jobs I was interested in were in the capital city, so here I was, a country girl stuck in the middle of the largest urban area in Britain.

I coped with it because of the little 'villages' that you find even in the biggest municipalities. For example, there was a real community spirit at the stables where I kept Leo; and Putney, where I lived, had a homely feel about it. Shopkeepers knew your name and neighbours actually spoke to you—like the Steadmans, the retired couple upstairs who always stopped for a chat, or Mrs Lacey, a widow from downstairs who regularly pressed home baking into my hands.

Work wasn't bad either—it was a big organisation, but having friends there made it more enjoyable.

As I descended the last few steps leading to Tower Hill tube station, an unearthly screech almost caused me to jump out of my skin.

"When did Dev get hold of my phone?" I grumbled, as I fished it out of my pocket. It was his favourite trick, to change my ringtone for something entirely inappropriate. I reckoned he'd been a pickpocket in a former life, as I was sure I hadn't left it unattended at the party.

It was Nicholas, my boss. "You went before I had time to say," he started, without preamble, "I'm calling a team breakfast meeting for eight a.m. on Monday. Something important has come up."

I made a face at the phone. Why couldn't he just have emailed? "No problem, see you then."

My finger was about to hit the red button when a tinny voice came out of the speaker. "Bring your incognito laptop."

Taken aback, I brought the device to my ear again. "Okay. Any hints what it's about?"

"You'll find out on Monday." The line went dead.

Computer scientists aren't exactly renowned for their people-skills, but Nicholas Spence took it to extremes. He was all about the work, no play—and something of a dull boy.

Shaking my head, I slid the phone into my inside pocket and headed through the barriers of the tube station.

Time for some horse therapy.

When I made it to the stables an hour later, I found several of the other horse owners already there and up to their elbows in straw and hay. Someone had brought mince pies, Christmas songs were playing on the radio, and there was an impromptu karaoke sing-along competition in progress.

Apparently Suzannah, whose horse was housed next to mine, had killed it with a rendition of *The Fairytale of New York*, using her pitchfork as a make-believe microphone stand.

I opened the door to Leo's stable—or stall, as Veronica, the American lady on the opposite side of the barn aisle would call it—and checked the state of his straw bed. I groaned. It looked like he'd been having his own party in there last night.

As I went off in search of a wheelbarrow, *Last Christmas* by Wham came on the radio, and Kirsty, three stables down, took to the floor. In the central passageway between the stables, she turned up the collar of her jacket in true eighties style, used her fingers to smooth her hair over her eyes, and sang soulfully into a grooming brush.

Needless to say, with such entertainment going on, my time at the yard passed in a twinkling. Soon Leo was tucked up in a nice clean stable with plenty of hay to see him through the night, and I was ready to head home.

Even though it was barely nine o'clock when I got home to my cozy flat in Putney, I was ready for bed. It'd been a long day—all that socialising at the Christmas party, and then the impromptu shindig with my horsey friends was quite wearing for a person like me who was something of an introvert. I generally preferred animals to people.

Then, tomorrow I had to get up at stupid o'clock to drive south for a training course. So an early night was in prospect.

It was only when I was almost asleep that I remembered the mysterious rhyme in my Secret Santa card. *It'll need to wait,* I thought groggily, then zonked out and headed for dreamland.

CHAPTER TWO

BUT I DIDN'T GET to think about the Secret Santa mystery until Sunday night. It was all Robert Redford's fault.

As a horsey teen, I'd watched his film, *The Horse Whisperer*, and become determined to learn to do some of the things he did. Through Pony Club and my long-suffering Connemara pony, Jangles, I'd experimented—with mixed results. But as an adult, once I got Leo, I'd realised I couldn't just muddle along. I needed to study it properly.

So I'd invested in a part-time course at a farm on the South Downs, which I'd been attending monthly for most of this year. And, as of this weekend, I was now a fully qualified 'Horsemanship' Trainer, skilled in using natural methods such as body language to guide and work with the horse.

It had been an intense couple of days, with borrowed horses to train, final lecture sessions to attend, and an exam to pass, but it was done, and I couldn't wait to tell Leo—even though it was dark and I hadn't eaten dinner yet.

Driving along the streets of Richmond, I marvelled at the number of Christmas trees covered in twinkling fairy lights that sparkled in the windows of the flats and houses I passed.

Shops and restaurants were decorated with fake snow or holly wreaths, the people on the street all seemed to be laughing, and my car radio was playing seasonal songs.

I smiled, feeling less like Grinch and more like Gonzo in the Muppets Christmas Carol. All I needed now was to sing carols at the Watchnight Service back home in Scotland, and I'd *really* be in the festive spirit.

With a sigh of satisfaction, I pulled my little red Corsa into the car park at the livery yard. Street lights gleamed orange on the road outside, but the lights were off in the stables, and all was quiet. Everyone else must have gone home.

Except—there was one car still parked up in the corner, a Mini, from what I could see. My good mood evaporated. Had someone had a riding accident and been taken off in an ambulance? *I guess I'll find out from the others tomorrow*, I said to myself.

Switching on the lights in the barn, I strode toward Leo's stable. A few sleepy noses turned my way, but most of the horses continued dozing or munching at their hay.

Leo was near the end of the building, and on the way I passed an empty stable, then stopped abruptly. A flash of colour had caught my eye. What could it be? I peered over the half door.

Blinking up at me from a sleeping bag resting on a thick bed of straw was Trinity Allen, one of the part-time grooms who worked at the yard. Her long dark hair was all mussed up, and her sand-coloured skin looked pale.

"Trinity! Sorry to wake you up. Have you got an early start for a competition or something?" Even as I said that, I realised that tomorrow was Monday, and horse shows were usually run at weekends.

She rubbed her eyes and swallowed. "Don't tell, will ya? I'll get into trouble from Mrs B if she finds out. It's just..." She screwed up her face. "I had to leave the flat. I've left Dwayne. But there weren't anywhere else I could think of to go. An' I was too scared to sleep in my car. Thought it would be warmer in here."

"Oh no, that's terrible!" Something about her forlorn look tugged at my heart strings. Trinity was one of the people I liked best at the stables, always cheerful, kind to the horses and a real bundle of energy. It was strange to see her despondent like this. "But you can't stay here—it'll be freezing later. Grab your stuff and you can sleep on my couch. It pulls out to make a bed."

"Aw, bless you, Izzy. But I don't want to be any trouble to ya. I've got a six thirty start tomorrow morning at the yard." She pulled her phone out of a pocket. "So I've set an alarm so I can tidy up my things before anyone gets 'ere."

"And I've a breakfast meeting at *my* work. So I'll be up at the crack of dawn too." I gave her a reassuring smile. "C'mon, you'll be much more comfortable at mine. Give me a minute to check on Leo and I'll be right with you."

Leo, to give him his due, stopped eating his hay and came over to the stable door. It was probably just greed, for he snuffled at my pockets, hunting for treats, but it made me feel like he appreciated my presence.

In an excited whisper, I told him about passing the course. He gazed at me with his soft brown eyes, then tilted his head, inviting me to itch his neck. Next thing I knew, my fingers were buried in the silky hair behind his ears, and he was bending into the scratch with an expression of pleasure on his face. With a laugh, I realised that my horse had probably trained *me* better than I had ever trained him—course or no course!

When Leo finally had enough of ear-rubs, I headed back to where I'd left Trinity. I gave her a sideways look. "Have you eaten? I was going to stop for a Chinese take-away on the way home."

Her brown eyes widened. Now that she was out in the light of the barn aisle I could see that they were red-rimmed, as if she'd been crying. "D'you know, that sounds good. I were too upset to be hungry earlier. But now me old stomach feels like me throat's had a knife taken to it."

Forty minutes later, we were sitting in the warmth of my rented flat, devouring king prawn chow mien and sweet chilli chicken with egg fried rice.

On the middle floor of a three-storey apartment building in the district of Putney in London, my home was small but serviceable. It had an open-plan living/dining/kitchen room which you entered from the shared corridor. To the right, inside the door, there was a shower room, and beyond that a separate bedroom large enough for a double bed, a wall of built-in wardrobes and not much else. The thing that had sold the place to me was the light—the flat was south facing and painted in pale shades with a fawn-coloured carpet through-out, so it always seemed bright and cheerful.

"Had you been with Dwayne long?" I asked Trinity, biting into a greasy prawn cracker.

"It's only been six months. But he's always been one of those jealous types." She put down her fork. "Tonight he came along to one of my salsa classes, I think he only went to check up on me. Well, he caught me chatting to one of the clients—one of the male ones. And, oh my word, did he lose his rag!" Her hands flew up expressively, and she almost knocked over her plate of food.

"He were ranting and raving about how I shouldn't be talking to other men and how he couldn't trust me and that I was a right—" she glanced across at me, "—well, let's just say he was angry. Very angry. But Winston—the lad I was talking to—he's got a girlfriend. He's been having dancing lessons to surprise her, like. So there was absolutely nothing in it, I told Dwayne that. But he wouldn't listen. He went and lost the plot."

"Sounds like he's a bit possessive."

"You're not wrong. An' it's not the first time he's been like that, neither. So off I went home, packed up me stuff and left before he could stop me."

She picked up her fork again and took a mouthful of chicken. "A girl I used to know, something similar happened to her; her bloke got really mean and controlling and she ended up in hospital. So there's no way I was having that happen to me. But I was so angry with him when I left that I hadn't really thought it through, and I hadn't worked out where I'd stay. Really stupid of me, I know. I'll have to start flat-hunting tomorrow."

She grimaced. "Although goodness knows when I can fit it in. I've got work at Mrs B's till four, and then from four thirty until nine I've got dance classes."

"You could have a look at lunchtime? On your phone?" I paused for a moment, realising that she wouldn't just walk into a new flat with half a day's notice. "But you can stay here for a few days till you find something, as long as you don't mind the couch."

"You're having a laugh. I couldn't do that."

"Well, if you can find a flat to rent tomorrow, then that's great. But it'll probably take a day or two to find one, won't it?"

"Yeah, I s'pose it might," she mumbled through a mouthful of rice.

"So stay here till you get somewhere else. It'll be nice to have a bit of company—though it sounds like you work most of the time so I won't see much of you, anyway." I jumped up and went over to a shallow cupboard by the door and returned clutching a key. "Here's my spare key. I go to the stables most nights after work, as you probably know; so I don't usually get back here until about eight. I'll cook a quick stir fry tomorrow and you can heat some up when you get in from dancing. After that you can just text me and we can arrange who cooks."

Her eyes glistened. "Aw, Izzy, you're so kind." She pointed at the cooker with her fork. "On a Tuesday I finish earlier, so it'll be my turn to cook *you* something. If I'm still here," she added.

"Deal!"

Stacking our plates together and grabbing the cutlery, Trinity headed for the kitchen nook, which was in a corner of the open-plan living area. "I'll wash up," she shouted over her shoulder, putting the dishes in the sink.

Unfolding my legs from under the dining table, I stood. "I'll dry then."

"Don't you dare! I'll be done in two shakes. You go and do what you'd normally do on a Sunday night."

"But you're my guest! You don't need to tidy up."

She threw her hands wide in an expressive gesture. "I do, y'know. I'm a compulsive cleaner. Blame my Italian mother. But it comes in handy when you work as a groom."

With a shrug, I turned on the TV. Flicking through the channels, all I could find were Christmas shows or Hallmark movies. "Do you want some escapism? Or shall I fire up Netflix?"

Wiping her hands in a dishtowel, Trinity squinted at the screen. "Dwayne and me had Sky, not Netflix. Is there anything good to watch?"

"Lots. I've been working my way through all the CSI episodes. How do you feel about good-looking Americans solving seemingly impossible crimes?"

"Now *that* sounds like my cup of tea. I tell you, right at this minute, I'm fed up to the back teeth with romance."

Half an hour later, when the detectives were up to their eyeballs in suspects, clues and dead bodies, I found myself wondering what Grissom would do, if he'd been given a rhyme by his Secret Santa.

With the gift card in one hand, I pulled out my laptop, fired up a search window and typed in 'The Secret'.

Various books, films, and lacy underwear sites were listed, but nothing that looked like it was anything to do with my note. Next, I tried 'Robin Hood 1454', and once more found links to films plus various pubs in England. But from the Robin Hood page on Historic England's website, I discovered that the green-clothed vigilante had probably been born in the twelfth century, or perhaps in the thirteen hundreds. Not fourteen fifty-four.

So what was the rhyme all about?

I squinted at the signature again. Were those letter Os or zeros? Robin Hood with numbers instead of letters was more like a password than a username. Frowning, I typed *that* into Google, but the search engine decided I couldn't spell and gave me the same results again. I sighed.

Trinity looked across at me from the armchair. "Everything all right?"

"Just..." I hesitated, wondering what to tell her. "I got a card from the Secret Santa at our office party, and it had a strange poem on it."

"Strange like weird, or strange like modern and not rhyming?"

Picking up the remote control, I paused Netflix. "Weird I suppose. I think it might be a clue to a mystery."

Her eyes lit up. "Y'mean a real live mystery?" She pointed at the TV set in the corner. "Like CSI?"

I pursed my lips. "Hopefully not! Probably a colleague was just playing a joke on me."

"Go an' read it to me?" she asked.

Studying her briefly, I reasoned to myself that she didn't work for Bleubank, so 'the secret you must keep' part probably wouldn't apply to her. Plus, it would be good to have someone to discuss it with. Clearing my throat, I picked up the card and read out the verses of the poem, then looked up at her. "What d'you think?"

She wrinkled her nose. "You work at a bank, don't you?"

I nodded.

"Well, what I think is, someone's doing something dodgy, and your Secret Santa thought you was exactly the person to work out what was going on."

"But why not just report whoever-it-is, if they know there's wrongdoing happening?"

"Maybe they only suspect something's going on. Or maybe they're not in a position to get proof, but they know that you are. What's your job again?"

"IT. Information Technology."

She tilted her head enquiringly, obviously expecting more.

"Computer Security Analyst. I test our systems," I raised a palm, "looking for weaknesses. Basically I'm a hacker. White-hat, they call us. Like in the cowboy movies, the villain always wore a black hat and the hero a white Stetson."

"Well, that must be it! There must be something in the security. Or the systems. Something that only *you* could find."

"But there's three on our team. Why not contact Dev? Or Manda?"

Trinity drummed her fingers on the arm of her chair. "P'rhaps they don't trust the others." She suppressed a smile. "You've an honest face. Or perhaps they *suspect* the others, but for some reason they've ruled you out."

I stared, unseeing, at my laptop, scrolling back through the last couple of weeks in my head, trying to remember when I'd been out of the office but the rest of the team were in. Or, conversely, when I'd been the sole person there. "Apart from lunchtimes, when we all dive out at different times to grab a sandwich, the only time I can think of recently that I wasn't at work but the others were, was last Friday afternoon when I took time off to wash and plait Leo ready for the dressage show at Windsor."

"P'rhaps that was it." She frowned. "Or maybe they just want to give you a mystery to think about, to stop you finding something else."

"You could spend forever thinking about all the options if you head down that route. I'll have a dig around at work tomorrow and see what I find." I picked up the remote and waved it at the telly. "Let's finish this episode and head to bed. We've both got an early start."

CHAPTER THREE

NICHOLAS SINCLAIR's idea of a breakfast meeting was for us to bring our take-away coffees while he provided a single bag of pastries from the nearest supermarket. His stinginess was infamous within Bleubank, and Dev and I had quickly learned to bring muffins or porridge as well as a hot drink.

Manda, however, had never been seen to eat, which might explain her bird-like figure. Instead of coffee, she sipped at a clear glass mug filled with boiling water and a slice of lemon.

My love for coffee was also infamous within Bleubank. Tucked in a back street, half-way between the tube station and the office was Caffè Fiorio, which, in my opinion, made the best coffee in the whole of London.

Giovanni, the owner, who considered Starbucks a thing of the devil, had succumbed to my pleading, and would grudgingly make me a take-away in my 'keep cup', warning me every morning to "not tell any of the other customers that I let you take my precious coffee away with you when you rush in here like a scirocco." Hands would fly expressively in the air. "Coffee from Caffè Fiorio should be savoured. You should sit, taste, appreciate!"

So every morning I would reply that his coffee tasted like nectar from the gods, and that he must be the finest barista in all of London, but that if I wanted to be able to afford my coffee habit, I needed to get to work rather than sit in Italian cafés.

Clutching my double-shot cappuccino, I would hurry to the office, then sip reverentially while the caffeine kick-started my brain.

Today was no exception.

Grunting "Good morning," to Dev and Manda, I entered the small second-floor meeting room. Bleubank prided itself on having ergonomic and productive workspaces. But what that really meant in practice was that the interior designers had picked office furniture in the company colours of airforce blue and silver, and arranged everything—apart from the meeting rooms—in an open-plan layout.

My preference was to sit opposite the window, so I could see the sky, and dream a little. London could feel claustrophobic at times; all concrete and glass high-rises, narrow streets, and crowds of people hurrying hither and thither.

I lived for the weekends, when I could ride Leo in Richmond Park, and pretend I was in the country—for a couple of hours at least.

I put my laptop and my cherished coffee on the table, close enough that the bittersweet aroma of the Colombian beans could filter its way into my neurons. Then I pulled a container with a blueberry muffin out of my messenger bag.

Across from me, Dev looked spritely as a spring lamb. He was obviously a lark, and the owl in me hated him—just for a second. It was too much effort, this early in the morning, to be annoyed at him for longer. In front of him sat a take-out cup of black tea.

Manda was sipping her customary lemon water, and wearing her customary black—black boots, black slacks and high-necked pullover, topped by a sheet of raven-glossy hair falling over one eye and hiding half her face. All she needed was a gun and she could audition for a James Bond movie.

Wondering whether she'd be a villain, accomplice or love interest kept me amused, briefly, until I realised that I, too, wore a sort-of uniform to work.

At my first job in Oxford, I'd come to the conclusion that a smart jacket could make Cheapside appear more like Chelsea. So I generally wore dark chain-store trousers or leggings with a self-coloured t-shirt and toning designer jacket which would give the whole outfit more class.

Today's jacket was almost military style, with double rows of brass buttons on a red, tartan-like wool weave. I'd bought it for next to nothing in the Jaeger closing-down sale last year, and it was one of my favourites for winter.

Dev started to ask how we'd enjoyed the Christmas lunch, but before we could get into any chit-chat about our weekends, the blue-painted door opened and Nicholas stalked in, carrying a tablet computer and the expected cheapo croissants. He placed them in the centre of the grey-blue melamine table, sat down, then looked at us over the top of a pair of horn-rimmed spectacles.

New, I thought. *Must be reading glasses.* They made him look more hipster than ever, with his scruffy beard, slouchy blazer and flannel waistcoat.

"Good morning everyone." He opened his tablet and pulled out a stylus. "Let's get right into it, so we can get back to our desks." With a forefinger, he pushed the specs up his nose, dabbed the stylus a few times at the screen of his device, then looked up at us again. "Can I get a quick update on where you are with your projects? Manda, let's start with you."

In clipped tones that were so quiet they had me wanting to push the 'plus' volume button, Manda told him that, "the work with the web team is going according to schedule; I am assisting them by testing the new forms for security issues. So far I have found twenty instances of insecure inputs for them to rectify."

Dev went next. "The phone app is getting close to having a release date, let me tell you." His voice rose in pitch. "It's looking amazing. The mobile team are pulling out all the stops. Me, I've been focussing on the encryption and the cellular traffic, making sure that malicious outsiders can't get access to the data. It's been pretty full-on."

Nodding slowly as his bony fingers pattered across his tablet screen, Nicholas pressed his lips together. "And Izzy?"

"I've been examining the network systems, searching for weak spots or external vulnerabilities that hackers could exploit. I've been coordinating with Rob Gosling."

"Progress?"

I shrugged. "How long is a piece of string? As soon as we find and patch one hole, another pops up. It's like painting the Forth Rail Bridge."

My Scottish idiom appeared to sail right over his head. "So you don't have any set milestones on that one?"

"I guess not. It's—"

He cut me off. "Okay, well I have a new task for you. Start date today." He glanced at Dev and Manda. "Thank you for your time. There's no need for you to wait while I explain this new project to Izzy."

Dev's bushy eyebrows crept up his forehead, but he meekly gathered his things and sloped out, followed by Manda.

Swivelling in his seat so he could face me better, Nicholas took off his specs and fixed his pale grey eyes on me. "We've received intel from our parent company in France that there have been some..." his mouth turned down, "irregularities in the internal systems. Nothing concrete, just a data delay here, a parity error there. There's concern that someone might have infiltrated our networks. There was a veiled comment on Twitter from the 404 Hacker Group which could have something to do with it."

My interest was piqued. "When was this?"

"On Friday when we were all at the party. You can check it out when you get back to your desk." He swiped the screen on his tablet, then raised his chin. "Any questions?"

"Um—do you have anything specific for me to go on?"

"I'm afraid not. You'll be looking for anomalies. Unexplained glitches. Inconsistent date tags."

"The ghost in the machine?"

For a moment he looked surprised. "Yes. You could call it that."

I chewed my lip. "Is there a deadline for my ghost busting?"

He scratched at his scraggy beard with a thumb. "Head office didn't say. But it would be helpful to have an answer for them before the holidays. After that I'll be busy with annual report data."

Two weeks. A fortnight to find a nebulous issue that mightn't even exist. *Joy.* "Couldn't it just be some rogue programming that's causing the errors?"

"Quite possibly. But it's your job to track it down."

Perhaps it was paranoia, but I was beginning to feel like the fall guy. "What happens if I don't?"

The stylus tapped emphatically on the edge of his tablet. "I have every faith in you."

In my head, I growled. His non-answer was typical management speak, and it annoyed the pants off me. I narrowed my eyes. "So I've fourteen days to find something that may or may not exist, that nobody else has been able to track down, with nothing really to go on? That's going to look good on my appraisal," I added sarcastically.

He had the grace to look sheepish. "This project is off the books, so you needn't worry in that regard. If you don't get any results by Christmas, then we'll re-assess."

I blew out a breath. "Is there someone to liaise with at head office? Or can they send me screenshots of the issues they've seen?"

"I'll put you in touch with Antoine Lanier in our Paris IT team. But you'll report directly to me, and you've to say nothing to anyone else in the department. This is strictly on the QT." He lifted his chin, indicating my laptop. "And work only on the incognito. Okay?"

Stalling, I took a slug of my coffee. Despite how impossible the task sounded, I was intrigued. It would be like *CSI-Information Technology*. Forensic detective work on our computer systems, hunting for dastardly hackers. I *liked* a mystery. So this might be fun? "All right, I'm in," I said with a nod of my head.

He smiled for the first time that morning. "Good." Picking up his tablet, he pushed his chair back. "I suggest you start on the dark web. See if you can find any references to Bleubank there. I'll catch up with you on Wednesday."

And with that, he was gone, the door swishing across the grey carpet and closing behind him with a muted thunk.

Absent-mindedly, I picked up my coffee and the untouched packet of croissants, thinking that I should be wearing grey coveralls with a big black backpack. "Who ya gonna call?" I said to myself and then giggled. *Antoine Lanier, naturally.* I hoped my schoolgirl French would be good enough.

* * *

Monsieur Lanier turned out to have excellent English. He was also rather charming, and much more encouraging than my boss. "Of course, of course, Mademoiselle Paterson. Anything for you. You are doing the important work, and I am told you have the unique skills to offer."

"Really?"

"Oui. Monsieur Spence thinks very highly of your investigation skills."

I blinked. Several times. "He does?"

There was a chuckle at the other end of the line. "I suppose he *can* be rather difficult to read. How you say? Stone face?"

"Yeah." That about summed him up. I could actually see the back of his head from where I sat.

We each had a relatively generous u-shaped arrangement of desks and shelves, with waist-height partitions between us. Nicholas was at the end, then Dev, me, and Manda at the other side.

"Well, okay, so I will send you the information I have. Although there is not very much. It will appear in your secure file transfer folder within the hour."

"Thanks, Monsieur Lanier, I appreciate your help."

Yawning, I leaned back and stretched. It was just after nine o'clock, and it felt like I'd done a day's work already. Reaching for my coffee, I up-ended the cup and swallowed the last of the cappuccino. I made a face. It had gone cold. *Might need another of those at lunchtime to keep my synapses firing.*

Normally, in circumstances like this, I'd make some sort of project plan. But if I wanted to keep things secret, I'd need to think of some way of keeping covert notes. I daren't write anything down.

But first, I had to keep myself busy until Antoine's files appeared. I drummed my fingers on the desk. Perhaps I could check out the Twitter lead that Nicholas had mentioned.

Using the incognito laptop, which automatically opened a secure connection to the internet, I logged in to Twitter with a disposable account. It didn't take long to find the hacker group's page. Scrolling back to their Friday tweets took longer, but eventually I found it:

> *Things are not as they seem in the world of*
> *corporate networks. #bleubank #security*
> *#cybersecurity #banking #finance*
> *#followthemoney*

Like Nicholas had said, it was pretty vague. And they hadn't directed the comment directly at Bleubank as if they wanted a response, they'd just hashtagged them.

On a whim, remembering my Secret Santa rhyme, I tried searching for Robin Hood and Robin Hood. *Nothing.* I chewed a thumbnail.

Perhaps I should check out the dark web, like Nicholas had suggested.

The dark web is a part of the world-wide-web that can't be searched by normal search engines. Everything that happens there is hidden by spaghetti-like layers of encryption, so it's pretty much impossible to trace who anyone is, or who is hosting information.

Of course, that makes it a great location for criminals selling contraband, or for scammers and hackers. But it also has a positive side, providing anonymous communications channels for people in countries where free speech is criminalised, or where governments eavesdrop on their citizens.

None of that was my concern right now, though. I needed to search for references to Bleubank. With a normal web browser on the dark web, this would prove impossible. Even with a specialist browser it was difficult. But I had a secret weapon—something nobody at Bleubank knew about. *Gremlin.*

Round my neck and tucked under my t-shirt hung a

quartz pendant, shaped like a teardrop. Taking it off, I flicked open the end, revealing a hidden USB flash drive which contained the Gremlin code.

Gremlin was an app I'd written as a university project; a search engine for the deep web. Exactly what I needed right now. It was versatile, too—it would also work like Google on the surface web, so, given the right keywords to look for, it would carry out a comprehensive search anywhere and everywhere. I inserted it into the laptop and set it going.

While Gremlin did its stuff, I had to keep busy, so I turned on the desktop computer which I used for the majority of my work, and opened up my email program.

My sigh was so loud it earned me a sharp look from Manda.

In the space of one weekend, how could there be ninety-six questions or pieces of information so important that someone had sent or copied them to me? My shoulders sagged.

The next half-hour was spent answering or filing emails (usually in the round bin), until Antoine's data arrived, rescuing me from my Inbox infinity. But his files had me scratching my head.

Everything he'd seen, all the weird issues—they were all in our *internal* systems. Nothing external. Nothing on the internet. So why did Nicholas have me wasting time on the dark web? I massaged my temples, my brain hurting.

Was it only because of that tweet by the 404 group? Or was he trying to throw me off the scent? I shook my head. But why, then, would he have asked me to look into this in the first place?

I decided I was just being paranoid. His reasoning must be that if an external hacker group had somehow got into our network, perhaps there would be a reference on the dark web. That made sense. So I'd leave Gremlin to it, and see what it turned up.

In the meantime, I should concentrate on our internal systems. But where to start?

Frowning, I clicked back to the hacker group's twitter feed. There was something nagging me about that.

It took a few minutes, but finally it dawned on me.

Follow the money.

They had hash tagged that, and it was also in the Secret Santa rhyme. So, did the person who sent me the riddle somehow know about the issues Nicholas and Antoine had uncovered? I rubbed my temples again.

"You look like you need a coffee." A loud voice startled me. *Dev,* peering over the partition between us like a meerkat in the desert.

I nodded theatrically and faked a yawn, whilst surreptitiously sliding a piece of paper over the side of my laptop to cover the Gremlin USB. "Yeah. Is it that time already?" I checked my watch.

"I'll go and put the kettle on." He indicated the unopened packet of croissants on my desk. "You bring the eats."

Grabbing my mug and the pastries, I followed him to the kitchen area at the end of our floor. From the cupboard I produced my pack of espresso and over-cup coffee filter, spooned grounds into the filter then poured boiling water on top, to percolate through. It wasn't Caffè Fiorio, but it was miles better than instant coffee.

His mug of tea made, Dev took a bite of croissant, then leaned back against the counter and tilted his head at me. "So, what is this mysterious project that Auld Nick has you working on?"

I thought quickly. "Nothing much. He's got me looking for data for the annual report. Just until Christmas."

That seemed to satisfy him. He brushed a crumb off his t-shirt.

"How's the phone app going?" I asked, to distract him from asking me any further questions about my work.

He pressed his lips together and rolled his neck. "It's looking good. Think we'll be done by the new year."

"And then what?"

His eyes took on a far-away look. "Then I'm thinking about moving on. Maybe back home to Ireland. PayPal are recruiting for their mobile app team in Dublin." He gave me a sideways glance. "I've sent in my CV."

I puffed out a breath. "Wow. I didn't see *that* coming."

He shrugged. "It's time. I've been here two years. To be honest, that's more than enough time in this place." One of his big hands swept through the air, indicating the blue and grey business landscape around us. "And I've had my fill of London, too. D'you know, in my local, they're charging a *fiver* for a pint of Guinness?" He sounded genuinely shocked at that.

"So you're going to leave me to cope with Manda and Nick all on my own, just because of the price of beer?" I teased.

Green eyes swivelled sideways. "You could always come too. There's more than one opening."

Wow. I didn't see that coming either.

To give myself time to think of a suitable answer, I busied myself getting milk out of the fridge and stirring it into my coffee.

"There are plenty horses in Dublin," continued Dev, "you'd love it. And keeping a horse in Ireland has got to be loads cheaper than it is over here."

A sip of my drink gave me another few seconds thinking time. Or recovery time. Dev had never given me anything except friendship vibes. But this sounded... more, and it was a lot to take in.

"I've never thought about moving to Ireland," I said, truthfully. "But you make a good point. And I've heard lots of positive things about PayPal. Let me know how you get on."

From under my eyelashes while I sipped my coffee, I examined Dev. Today's t-shirt was emblazoned with the batman logo. Baggy blue jeans and Nike trainers completed the ensemble. It was only on the worst days of winter that he added a denim jacket on top, seeming impervious to the cold.

Curling at the back of his neck, his black hair was messy as ever and slightly too long. On the plus side, Dev *did* have nice eyes and a friendly smile, but I'd never thought of him as anything except a colleague and friend, especially since relationships with people at work were usually a bad idea.

However, if I was reading his body language correctly, my non-answer seemed to have disappointed him. With feigned cheerfulness, he picked up his mug of tea and raised it in my direction. "I'll let you know. Now, I'd better press on."

"Me too," I said as he turned away.

I stared at his retreating back, wondering if I'd done the right thing. Did I want to stay in London, or would I consider a move to Ireland? Irish people always seemed lovely and friendly, in a 'talk the hind leg off a donkey' sort of way. And there was nothing in particular keeping me in the capital city, other than work opportunities.

But... Did Dev want more than friendship? It certainly felt that way, and any indication I gave that I was thinking about Dublin might encourage him, and that wouldn't be fair.

Wandering back to my desk, coffee in hand, I decided to put it behind me for now. I had enough else to think about— Secret Santas, temporary flatmates, horsemanship training and organising things so I could get home to Scotland for Christmas with my family. Not to mention mysterious data glitches at work. Surely that was more than sufficient for one person to be worrying about?

And then I smiled. Perhaps Gremlin would have found me the answer already, and I could tie everything up with a nice neat bow, then hand it over to Nicholas in time for Christmas.

It was a nice dream, while it lasted...

CHAPTER FOUR

THE CAFFEINE in my coffee seemed to be doing the trick. Gremlin was still busy hunting through the nether regions of the internet, but while it was occupied, I'd put my thinking cap on. I had worked out that an old-fashioned paper notebook would work for my secret project notes, as long as I always kept it with me. Even if hackers were on our internal systems, they wouldn't be able to read my notes, so they wouldn't know I was after them.

To that end, and remembering the 'follow the money' exhortation, I was mapping out a diagram of where the money went within Bleubank. And how it got there. And then how it passed *out* of Bleubank. The page on my notebook soon filled up with lots of boxes, and even more arrows. But, basically, it gave me two choices of where to start: either inside or outside the company.

I tapped my pen against my bottom lip as I thought it through.

Inside Bleubank made more sense—it would be easier, for one thing, and it seemed more likely, from what I'd found in Antoine's files.

The right tool for the job was a 'network sniffer'—an app that would run in the background and monitor the information travelling between the computers in our company. I could see which devices were involved, and check if anything looked anomalous. Maybe that would be all I'd need.

From our company software library, I downloaded Smart-Net, an app which promised to do just what I needed, and set it going. I'd probably need a full twenty-four hours of information to be sure I hadn't missed something, but I could extract the results hourly while I was in the office and at least get started.

Straightening my back, I pursed my lips and surveyed the technology around me. With the laptop busy, I needed to find something else to do, and I knew just what that should be. *The Secret Santa rhyme.*

It wasn't strictly a work thing, but the 'follow the money' coincidence had me wondering. Could the Antoine's Anomalies project and the Christmas Party Conundrum be related?

Pulling the gift card out of my bag, I stared at the verses, remembering my discussion with Trinity last night. Might something have happened on that Friday afternoon over a week ago, when I was away at the horse show?

Clicking on the Files app on my desktop computer, I chose the top-level which showed all the files on our network, and arranged them in date order. I checked the calendar hanging on my partition to find the date I needed, then concentrated on files changed on Friday the first of December in the afternoon.

There were a lot. Too many to investigate quickly. But hadn't Trinity suggested it might be something to do with Dev or Manda? I cut my eyes right and left, to check they weren't looking at me, then filtered the results by username. It showed two files modified by Manda, and none by Dev.

I couldn't stop myself glancing at Manda again. It was

illogical, since she'd have no idea what I was doing, and was probably busy with her own work, but I just wanted to be sure she wasn't watching me while I opened the files. She wasn't. Eyes fixed straight ahead at her screen, and frowning in concentration, her fingers flew across her keyboard.

Taking a deep breath, I clicked on the first of the files. It looked like it contained a bunch of test inputs for web forms, snippets of data similar to those a hacker might use.

The second file contained only streams of nonsensical letters and numbers. I scrolled through it, but could see no pattern, no rhyme or reason for the unintelligible contents. I was sure that file was unrelated, but, just in case, I used a USB flash drive to transfer a copy of it to the incognito laptop.

To my left, Dev was humming tunelessly under his breath, head bobbing slightly from side to side as he listened to music via a set of red Bluetooth headphones. Unfortunately, the absence of files by him didn't let my friend off the hook, as it was always possible they'd been edited again at a later date, therefore the date on the file would have been updated.

However, call me biased, but Dev didn't strike me as the sort of person who'd do anything nefarious. How could someone who looked like a cross between a brown bear and a character from The Lord of the Rings do something criminal?

I half-rose from my seat to attract his attention, then waited till he pulled the headphones off. "Sounds of the eighties?" I asked.

He made a clownish face. "I wasn't singing along again, was I?"

"You call that singing?" I teased.

If he'd rolled his eyes any harder, he'd have strained a muscle. "Do you not have a Christmassy bone in your body, Izzy Paterson? Surely even a philistine like you must like Band Aid?"

"Do I know it's Christmas?" I quoted the charity super-group's Christmas song title.

He put one forefinger on his nose and pointed the other at me. "I see what you did there."

I tilted my head at him. "I'll have you know I was singing Mariah Carey karaoke on Friday night at the stables."

His eyebrows climbed under his fringe. "I didn't know you sang."

"I don't." I grimaced. "Normally. But all the other girls were singing, so it felt churlish not to." I didn't tell him that I'd done a duet with Emma, and that she had done most of the *actual* singing, while I did a brilliant job of lip-synching. Much as I love music, I can't carry a tune to save my life.

"That's it settled then." He waved over the partitions at Manda until she looked up. "Works night out. Friday. Christmas karaoke. You up for it?"

She did that shaky-noddy head thing that means maybe-yes, maybe-no.

Dev gave her a thumbs-up. "I'll check out which pub is doing karaoke and let you know where." He checked to his left, but Nicholas must've gone without us noticing. "I'd better ask Nick, too."

"And the web team. Won't be much fun with only the four of us," I added.

"Grand idea," he said. "Let's make it so."

It was my turn to roll my eyes. "You're such a Trekkie."

He grinned. "And don't you just love me for it."

———

ANOTHER HOUR LATER, Gremlin had uncovered nothing unusual or suspicious about Bleubank on the internet, dark web or otherwise. With a growl of frustration, I sat back in my chair. I hadn't really expected it to find anything, but it was still annoying.

Dev peered over the partition. "You look like you need lunch."

"Is it that time already?"

"Can be."

"What I want is coffee. Again. Caffè Fiorio for me."

"You need to get an intravenous drip of that stuff."

A smile crept across my face. "Maybe Santa will bring me one."

He rolled his eyes for about the ninetieth time that day. "Paterson, get your coat. You're getting delirious. I prescribe some caffeine. Stat!"

I went to the Italian café perhaps once a week for lunch. Sitting at one of the tiny round tables dotted around the room, I would people-watch the variegated representatives of humanity who rushed past the window. It was almost soothing.

In front of me would be a bicerin: layered espresso, hot chocolate and milk, or, in warmer weather, a macchiato: espresso with a dash of steamed milk. Something to taste and appreciate. Something to keep Giovanni happy. Today was a bicerin day.

Because it was mainly a coffee shop, the food menu was limited. But the Italian owner made a mean caprese panini with avocado basil pesto. I ordered one of those, while Dev, not being a vegetarian, went for the Tuscan chicken.

We found a table by the window and had just begun to eat when a familiar figure walked past.

Walter Oxley, our Chief Financial Officer, came into the café wearing a well-tailored grey suit, clutching a tablet computer in his hand, and carrying a raincoat over his arm.

My brows scrunched as I looked up at the sky outside. "No sign of rain," I said to Dev. "Oxo must be a Boy Scout."

Dev followed my gaze. "Or maybe he feels the cold. He's a bit of a stick insect."

"True. The man makes size zero supermodels look fat."

Mr Oxley gave his order at the counter, then found himself a table opposite, putting his coat on one of the two empty chairs. He didn't seem to have noticed us, but I doubted he would recognise us anyway—we were mere plebs to such an exalted executive in the company management.

Placing a pair of half-moon reading glasses on his long nose, he propped his tablet case open and started tapping on a little Bluetooth keyboard.

"Can't leave his work behind," I commented as I took another bite of panini, then licked a dribble of pesto off my finger.

"Well, I'm glad you managed to," said Dev. "You were looking a bit fraught, back there. Is it *that* difficult to find info for the annual report?"

I shook my head. It pained me to lie to him, so I tried to tell the truth without revealing my secret project. "It's not that, it's just a bit..." I twisted my lips as I tried to think of the right word, "frustrating. Well, I suppose identifying the data *is* proving to be a bit of a problem. But I've got a couple of weeks."

"Sure. When are you finishing for Christmas?"

"A week on Friday. I'm at a dressage competition on the Saturday morning, then I've got train tickets back up to Scotland late afternoon. What about you?"

"I'm finishing the Friday lunchtime, then flying from Gatwick to Dublin that afternoon." He lifted his cup, as if toasting invisible companions. "I should be in the Dancing Leprechaun with the boys by eight."

"Maybe you can organise an interview with PayPal while you're over."

"That's the plan," he said, cutting me a look.

Realising I'd moved the conversation onto difficult ground, I looked across at Mr Oxley again, hoping to change the subject. Then I jerked my head back in surprise. "Oxo has a friend."

Dev glanced over at the CFO's companion. "I don't recognise him."

"Me either."

The man that had joined the big boss was about half his age and half his height. Wearing a dark suit and tie, he had short auburn hair and a tidy beard, narrow eyes and a wide mouth. Something about him set my spidey senses tingling.

Mr Oxley had closed his tablet when the other man arrived, and now they were in earnest conversation, almost head-to-head across the table. They were interrupted when the waiter arrived with the CFO's order—a bowl of soup, from what I could see. After a few words with Oxo's companion, the waiter disappeared back to the kitchen, and the two suits resumed their pow-wow.

A loud 'ping' had Dev retrieving his mobile.

Across the room, two heads turned, and the CFO and his friend stared at us for a second, before continuing their conversation.

My jaw tightened, and I wriggled my shoulders. It seemed we weren't anonymous plebs after all.

Dev checked his phone screen, then stuffed the last bite of panini into his mouth. "We should get back to the office. There's a staff meeting at two, it totally slipped my mind. It's as well I set a reminder."

"I'd forgotten too." I set about finishing my food, drained the dregs of my coffee, then followed Dev to the door of the café.

Before I left, I looked across at Mr Oxley's table. He was on his own again, and slurping the remains of his soup. Presumably he was also heading back to the office for the two o'clock session. "I guess we'll see him there," I said to Dev's retreating back.

———

IT TURNED out that Mr Oxley was one of the main speakers at the staff meeting. A monthly event which was supposed to help morale and communications within the company, they gathered nearly one hundred staff into the large atrium area on the ground floor of our building.

With grey marble floors throughout, boxy navy couches sat on each side of a square blue rug near the reception desk, then further over, a chrome staircase spiralled up to the higher levels. Apart from doors to the lifts, stairs and toilets, most of the rest of the concourse was open-plan, and ideal for a large gathering.

Mr Dempsey tapped the microphone, then cleared his throat. Behind him, our corporate logo was being projected onto a large screen which hung from the ceiling. "Colleagues," he said, calling the session to order, "welcome to our December staff meeting. You'll be pleased to hear it's a short agenda today. Now, I hope you all enjoyed the Christmas lunch on Friday?" Pinning a fleshy smile to his face, he waited for our murmurs of agreement, before signalling for the next slide.

Up popped one of those ubiquitous jaggy charts that looks like it's showing someone's heart rate, but is actually displaying profits. Or losses. This graph had a significant droop at the end. If it'd been my heart, I'd have been off to the hospital.

"I'm going to call on our CFO, Mr Walter Oxley, to talk to you about company performance," continued Dempo, opening an arm to invite Mr Oxley to the mic.

"Ahem. Ladies and gentlemen, good afternoon." Oxo's

voice was as thin and reedy as his body. He waved an arm at the graph behind him. "As you will see from this diagram, whilst profits were robust in the first quarter of the year, things have declined since then, and we are looking at a significant shortfall in this current period."

He was so tall that he had to hunch his shoulders to speak into the microphone. "We have a shareholder meeting next week, so you can rest assured that your management team is pulling out all the stops to address the issues before then."

"What *are* the issues?" Someone called from the middle of the crowd. It sounded like Rob Gosling, but I couldn't see.

A brief look of irritation crossed Mr Oxley's face. "Ahem. I'll take questions at the end. But, to answer your question, company performance has declined, and we are looking to improve it."

"Is that not what he just said?" I said under my breath.

"Obfuscation worthy of a politician," Dev whispered back.

At the front, Oxo signalled for the next slide. It was a pie chart, with a few large slices and one tiny sliver. "Now, as most of you will be aware, this is the time of year when we usually award staff bonuses."

That word, 'usually', caught my attention. Judging by the stirring and murmuring in the assembly, I wasn't alone in that.

"As you can see," the CFO used a pen to point at the pie chart, "once we have covered our salary commitments, fixed costs and shareholder remunerations, there is almost nothing left this year for bonuses."

The murmuring increased to muttering.

In most other areas of business, workers got paid every week or month, and were happy with that. But the financial services industry had a tradition of paying annual bonuses, and staff had begun to expect that—even to rely on it. For most of my colleagues, to hear that the payout would be reduced was bad news indeed. Especially this close to Christmas.

Since I'd not worked for Bleubank that long, I'd not begun to rely on the bonuses. Fortunately. In the last couple of weeks, I had to admit to drooling over websites with fancy new bridles for Leo, and smart competition jackets for me. But I didn't *need* them, so I'd be fine either way.

Mr Oxley cleared his throat again. "Your managers will meet with you in the next forty-eight hours and let you know individually what you can expect in your December pay packet." He lifted his chin. "Now, I thank you for your time. Let's all get back to work and get those profits rolling in again!" With that he turned away, hurried over to the lifts with Mr Dempsey, and they disappeared up to the management suite in the top floor like rats scurrying up a drainpipe.

Around us, more than a few jaws had to be lifted off the ground. "So much for taking questions at the end," I said, still trying to process what I'd just witnessed.

"I guess that's my new car out the window," said Dev with a mock sigh. "I'll not be able to impress the girls with my wheels after all."

"If all it takes to impress the girls is a fancy car, then they're probably not the sort of girls you'd actually want," my logical side replied before my tactical brain had time to approve the comment.

"You're so right," he said, flashing me a look from under his eyelashes.

Uh-oh.

"We'd better get back to work," I said brightly, unsubtly changing the subject, "and get those profits rolling in again, like the man said."

CHAPTER FIVE

THE MEMORY of the declining profits chart haunted me all afternoon as I examined spreadsheets filled with SmartNet results. Was the poor corporate performance the *real* reason behind the tricky task Nicholas had set me? Or were hackers somehow siphoning off our profits? I scratched my head. But surely the company auditors would pick up on that?

Unless... perhaps the hackers were getting to the money before it got as far as our accounts? Could they surreptitiously divert funds before we'd even counted them, and therefore our accountants hadn't missed them? I'd need to do some more research on that one. But it could wait until tomorrow.

With a start, I realised that the office around me was quieter and darker than usual. Several staff had already gone home, but I'd been so caught up in my analysis of the figures that I hadn't noticed.

Glancing at the clock in the corner of my computer screen, I reckoned that, if I hurried, I'd be able to get to the stables by seven thirty. Then I could ride quickly before tucking Leo up for the night.

Locking the incognito laptop into the deep drawer at the bottom of my desk, I pushed my notebook into my cross-body bag, tucked the Gremlin necklace under my shirt, checked my phone was in my pocket, then grabbed my coat and rushed off down the stairs.

On my way across the concourse to the main doors, I was joined by Rob Gosling from the networks team. "You're not heading for the tube station, are you?" he asked. About the same height as me but significantly wider, he was the sort of man whose glass never even got to half full.

Working with him on the network security project, the only way I'd coped with his relentlessly negative attitude was to get him talking about one of his passions: birdwatching on the Norfolk Broads, or playing Fortnite on his PlayStation. He seemed a solitary man, obsessed with his gadgets and technology.

"Yeah. If I hurry, I'll catch the six ten."

He pushed up his sleeve and checked his Apple watch. "I'll probably miss my train. But I may as well walk with you."

"Of course." The automatic doors opened before us, and we strode out into the rush hour.

"Spence said you'd been reallocated." Street lights reflected off his large glasses as he glanced sideways at me.

"Yeah, he's got me gathering data for the annual report." A cold wind was whistling through the high buildings surrounding us. Fishing in my bag, I pulled out a black beanie, then wrapped my scarf tighter around my neck.

Power-walking to the nearest tube station, we joined hundreds of business-suited lemmings, dodging traffic and skipping round the occasional slow-moving tourist who blocked our way.

Overhead, multi-coloured Christmas decorations were strung across the street, and fairy lights twinkled in the windows of most of the shops we passed. It was a shame

London seldom got snow, because, if it had, the whole scene would have become quite festive.

Rob pulled a shapeless dark green hat over his thick black hair. "I'm thinking about writing to the papers about them doing us out of our bonuses. It's just not good enough. Them executives in their fancy offices with their six-figure salaries won't suffer a jot. But us poor sods who work hard for a living, we're the ones who're out of pocket."

How could I respond to that? I risked a quick glance at him and nearly crashed into a lamppost. Staggering slightly until I regained my balance, I tried something noncommittal. "Um, does anyone still read the papers? I thought it was all online petitions and FaceBook memes these days."

His face brightened. "A petition might be an idea." I could almost see the cogs whirring. "We could present it at the shareholder's meeting. Embarrass the fat cats."

We. I hoped he meant the royal 'we', because I didn't want to get involved in organising his protest. "There are plenty of online apps you could use to set up your petition." I said. I didn't emphasise the word 'your', but I hoped he'd take the hint.

"I'll look into it when I get home." He checked his watch again. "One hundred steps per minute." There was a brief pause while his lips moved silently. I guessed he was doing some mental arithmetic. "We need to increase to one-ten if you want to catch your train." With that he put on a spurt, dashed across a pedestrian crossing, and I almost lost him.

When we finally arrived at Monument Underground Station, I was breathing hard and had pulled off my hat and scarf. But I did catch the ten past six.

I never did find out if Rob made his train.

From my work to the stables it was about an hour's ride south west on the District Line, with a ten-minute walk at each end. To keep me entertained on the tube, I'd usually either read—if I got a seat—or listen to audio books if the service was busy and I ended up strap-hanging.

Recently, I'd been borrowing audio versions of the Hamish Macbeth mysteries from the library. They were well performed by the narrator and did a good job of describing the people and scenery in the far north of Scotland. But they also made me feel a little homesick for the open spaces and freedom of the Scottish countryside. I couldn't wait to be back with my family for Christmas.

When I arrived at the livery yard, I found my neighbour, Suzannah, busy grooming her horse, Cracker. She had him tied outside her stable and almost blocking the central aisle.

Short and cuddly with a mop of curly brown hair, Suzie Wilks was one of those 'salt of the earth' people without whom the country would fall apart. Working shifts as a nurse at a local children's hospital, she would arrive at the yard at all sorts of odd times, so we didn't often see each other, despite having next-door stables.

Squeezing past behind them, I kept an eye on the black horse's ears, which would give me the first warning sign of an impending kick. Not for nothing was he known in the barn as Cranky Cracker.

"Evening, love. How d'you get on at that course at the weekend?" Suzie asked, in her broad Manchester accent.

I reached Leo's stable without getting booted by Cracker. "Good thanks. I passed." Leo came to the door, and I touched my hand to his nose in greeting.

"Oh, that were mint." Suzie brushed behind Cracker's elbow. Obviously it was a sensitive bit, as she did well to dodge his teeth. She growled at him to behave, then asked me, "What'cha up to tonight?"

"Practicing my dressage test. We've got the final competition in the Parkside League a week on Saturday." Opening my stable door, I gave Leo a pat on the shoulder then tied his head collar on.

She puckered her forehead. "How's that work, love?"

"It's a series of dressage shows. You get points each time depending on your placing, and they get added up to find who the overall winner is."

"Oooh. I'm on nights that weekend, otherwise I'd have come to watch. How're you getting on?"

"Pretty good thanks. We're second overall at the moment. But the lady in third place is only a point behind, so it could go either way."

"Excitin'." She put down the brush she was holding and picked up a comb for his mane. "Well, all the best. I hope you win."

"Unlikely," I said, stepping out of the stable. "But thanks." Rummaging in my own grooming kit, I hunted for a hoof pick. "What're you up to yourself, tonight?" Spying the implement I wanted, I grabbed it and went back into my stable.

"Oh, nowt. Just a bit of pampering for his lordship here." She looked fondly at the crotchety gelding. Suzannah was one of those people who seemed to spend hours fussing over her horse, giving him the best of care and attention, but never actually riding.

Me, I enjoyed riding Leo so much that I'd exercise him pretty well every day, even though it meant early starts, late nights and not much of a social life. But my friends at the stable yard made up for it. We were quite the little community, and I relished my time there.

"Actually," Suzie called me over, "go an' have a look at this for me?" She motioned at something on Cracker's shoulder.

Nodding, I went back out to the aisle, putting a hand on the dark horse's flank as I passed him so he'd know I was there. All of a sudden, I felt a cramping pain in my gut, which almost had me doubled over.

"You okay, love?" Suzie's forehead creased in concern.

It took a moment to feel normal again. I breathed out heavily, then straightened. "Just a sore tummy. Must've been the panini I had for lunch." But that sparked an idea. Sticking my hands in my pockets, I contemplated Cracker's pinned back ears and swishing tail. "Suzie, did you ever think to get him checked for ulcers? That might explain his grumpy behaviour."

Her frown deepened. "You think?" She ran her eyes over her horse, as if trying to see beneath the surface. "You know, you could be right. That could be a reason for his quirky character." Her face cleared. "I'll phone the vet in the morning." Pointing at his shoulder, she added, "I could get them to look at that, too."

Glancing at the mark on Cracker's shoulder, I was able to reassure Suzie. "It's only a rub from his blanket. Often happens with sensitive-skinned horses in the winter. You don't need to bother with the vet for that—you can buy a shoulder guard for him to wear under his rug if it bothers you."

Once Leo was ready, I took him into the schooling area, mounted, then walked him round to warm us both up. After that I started working on exercises that would make him stronger and more supple, finally moving on to practicing the specific movements we'd have to perform at the competition.

Despite the cold, when we'd finished we were both sweating a little. Walking for five minutes helped to cool him off, then I took him back to his stable, gave him a feed, and wrapped him in a fleecy rug which would keep him warm overnight.

As the crow flies, it was only a few miles from the livery yard to my flat. The route went through Richmond Park, which, whilst very green and pleasant in the daytime, wasn't the safest place to walk alone in the dark. Because of that, I tended to drop my car at the yard in the morning so I could drive back safely at night.

After a short diversion via a local supermarket to pick up supplies for the stir fry I'd promised to make for Trinity, I arrived home. Throwing the ingredients into a wok, I sautéd the veg with one hand while the other used the remote to click through the channels on the TV. I finally settled on a re-run of a *CSI New York* episode.

When I at last heard Trinity's key in the lock, the delicious aroma of the Thai red curry sauce was making my stomach rumble.

"Good timing!" I said, pulling a couple of plates out of the cupboard. Then I caught sight of her face. "What's wrong?" I set the dishes on placemats before hurrying over to help her with the myriad of bags she held in either hand.

"Dwayne," she said, succinctly, a tear running down her cheek.

"Put those down," I inclined my head at her luggage, "take your coat off and sit yourself at the table. You can tell me all about it over dinner. You'll feel better with some food inside you."

She nodded mutely and did as I asked.

The whole sorry tale came out over the spicy vegetable curry. With a hitch in her voice, she told me how her final dance class of the evening had been cancelled because of a blocked toilet, of all things, so she'd decided to go to the flat she'd shared with Dwayne to pick up the remainder of her stuff.

Dwayne was out when she arrived, but returned just as she'd packed the last bag, reeking of beer and still wearing his work clothes. Barring the doorway, he demanded to know what she was doing.

Her hands flew in the air as she described their conversation. "'I'm getting my things,' I said to him. 'I told you I was moving out.'

"Then he said that I couldn't, that I still needed to pay half of next month's rent—my half. Well, I tell you, I could've seen him far enough. 'I've already paid for next month,' I told him. But he got all stroppy, like, an' shouted at me, 'Yeah but you have to give a month's notice.'

"Then he wouldn't listen to me when I told him it was four weeks' notice we needed to give, not a full month, and that it was only a few days ago that I paid a whole month up front. Apparently, he says I'm two days short of the four weeks' notice, and he just won't move an inch."

Her face crumpled. "And that's not the worst of it. If I 'ave to pay another month at that place, I won't have enough money left over to put down a deposit on a new flat."

I put my elbow on the table and tapped a thumb on my lip while I thought about it. "What job does he do?" I asked.

"He's a security guard at a store on Oxford Street."

"Does he use FaceBook?"

She nodded, swallowing another mouthful of curry.

"What's his full name and where's he from?"

"Dwayne Brooks. Dwayne Jeffrey Brooks. Born on an estate in Hackney I think."

"And his date of birth?" I grabbed a pen and paper so I could write it down.

She told me his birthday and age.

"And his mobile phone number?" I wrote that down too. "Okay, leave it with me and I'll see what I can find."

With the TV in the corner showing another CSI episode and the log-effect electric fire keeping the chill of night at bay, we sat in companionable silence in the living area. But I wasn't really paying attention to the telly.

Instead, I was curled on the couch with my laptop computer

on my knee—my personal one, not my work one—doing some digging into Dwayne's background. With Gremlin's help, and the information Trinity had given me, I was doing a bit of social media snooping to find out more about my friend's ex.

It only took me about an hour to hit the jackpot. "Gotcha!" I cried, and grinned over at Trinity.

She creased her brow at me. "What's up?"

"Jasmin Alisha Freeman updated her relationship status on FaceBook."

Trinity shook her head. "And I should care because...?"

"Because she's Dwayne Jeffrey Brooks' new girlfriend."

"No!" Her eyes widened. "The rat." Her voice got louder. "The skunk. The total toad." She rocketed out of her chair and stomped around the room, muttering under her breath and calling him every name under the sun.

I let her work off some steam. Then I prepared to tell her the coup de grâce. "Not only that, Trinity, there's more."

She spun round to look at me, eyebrows at sharp angles.

"Jasmin posted a photo this evening, of 'her new pad'." I turned my laptop so she could see the screen. It showed a tower block flat in Kingston, with Dwayne leaning against the door jamb, a cocky expression on his face.

That set off a fresh round of name-calling.

Unfolding my legs, I went to put on the kettle while I waited for her to calm down again. By the time steam had stopped coming out of her ears, I'd made two mugs of hot chocolate. She came to join me at the kitchen counter.

"You know what, Izzy, you're a genius."

I pushed a mug in her direction.

She picked it up and took a sip. "Thanks. But, listen, you was so quick, it were no time at all, like the blink of an eye before you found that out. It were like magic." Brown eyes locked onto mine. "You should do that for a living, girl. Izzy

Investigates. Richmond Research." Her lips twitched. "Or perhaps: Paterson's Probes."

Her last suggestion made me laugh out loud. "That sounds like something unmentionable they'd do to you in hospital."

She grinned. "Could be you're right. But, think about it. There must be millions of wives out there trying to find out what their rotten husband is up to. Or bosses wanting to check on new staff. You'd get loads of business."

"I like my current job." I lifted my shoulders. "But thanks." Placing my mug of hot chocolate back on the bench, I raised a hand. "We're not finished there, though. What time d'you finish work tomorrow? And when will Dwayne finish?"

"Now, let me think." She tapped her forefinger on her thumb. "The shops open late for Christmas shopping this week. So he should be at Macbie's till seven. Then home about eight if 'e don't go to the pub again. Me, I finish at six on Tuesdays. I said I'd cook, remember?"

I pursed my lips. "Okay, I'll ride Leo in the morning, then aim to get here maybe six thirty after work. Once we've eaten, we're taking a trip over to see Mister Brooks."

"We are?" She opened both hands. "Why would we want to do that? The man's a rotten, two-timing, lowlife scum of the highest order."

"I'll tell you tomorrow." I tapped the side of my nose. "But keep it quiet—we don't want him to find out you're onto him."

CHAPTER SIX

THINGS AT WORK the next morning were quieter than usual. Dev was away all day at an Apple developers' conference with the mobile app team, Nicholas was also out at some management briefing, and Manda had her headphones on and was engrossed in whatever she was looking at on her screen.

With my take-out coffee to oil the cogs in my brain, I spent most of the morning examining the SmartNet results. I was thinking about putting that to one side and doing some Secret Santa investigating, when Nicholas arrived back in the office and stopped by my desk.

"Any progress?" he asked, direct and to the point as usual.

I sighed heavily. "Nothing concrete so far, sorry. I've got a network sniffer monitoring our internal data traffic, which takes quite a lot of analysis, but it hasn't thrown up anything. Yet," I added.

"What about the dark net?"

"Drew a blank there. But everything Antoine sent seemed to be internal, so I think I need to focus here," I waved an arm in a circle to indicate the Bleubank building, "rather than outside."

A flash of something crossed his face, so quickly that I wasn't quite sure what I saw—possibly fear? But then his usual stony mask slipped back into place.

Keeping an eye on his expression, I added, "If there are hackers getting into our system, then the sniffer should pick that up."

He nodded, giving the briefest of smiles. "Yes. Sounds like you're on the case. Keep it up." And with that, he strode off to his desk.

I narrowed my eyes at his retreating back. Suspicion furrowed my brow. Could he have something to do with the hacking? But then, why would he have put me onto this task?

Unless... Could he have been ordered to allocate a member of his team to this project? Was I some kind of patsy?

Had he not told me specially to bring my incognito laptop to Monday's meeting? And yet none of the others had computers there. It was like he'd already decided, on Friday night when he phoned, that he'd give the job to me.

Perhaps he hoped I would fail, and he'd get away with— whatever it was he was up to. With a groan of frustration, I glowered at Nicholas' hunched shoulders and bent head, which was all I could see of him from here.

This task had me searching for shadows, suspicious of everyone and anything. What I needed was some kind of clue, or better still an answer, so I'd know what was *actually* going on and could work out who was responsible.

Maybe the thing to do was to have a break for lunch, clear my head, and then go through what I knew so far and try to make sense of it. Pushing myself up out of my chair, I headed for the kitchen area.

Once the kettle had boiled, I made a cup of coffee and headed back to my desk. Delving in my bag, I found the sandwich I'd bought on the way into work, ripped open the packaging and took a bite.

The tuna and sweetcorn roll was fairly unexciting, but while I ate it, I decided to check out Dwayne and Jasmin's social media again.

What I discovered nearly made me laugh out loud. Jasmin had posted another selfie of her with Dwayne, this time obviously taken in bed before they got up.

It amazed me that people would leave their FaceBook posts as public, in this day and age. Surely she should realise that *anyone* could see it? Anyway, there was no way Dwayne could deny their relationship now, so that would help Trinity's cause.

I spent a little while preparing some documents for our show-down with Dwayne that night, and then it was time to get back to work. Or rather, back to my investigations.

From my bag, I pulled out the Secret Santa card. It was starting to look somewhat dog-eared. I looked from the type-written rhyme to the laptop screen, wondering, once again, if the two mysteries were connected.

On a whim, I opened the most recent file of SmartNet results, and searched for 'The Secret'. Nothing. Then I tried 'Robin Hood'. Still nada. 'Robin Hood' with zeroes was next, and suddenly I got a result!

Leaning forward, I stared at the screen, hardly believing my eyes. Did I *finally* have a breakthrough on this case?

"Hello?" said a loud voice.

I just about jumped out of my skin. Spinning round, I came face-to-face with Frank Varley. Well, face to chest, to be precise. I looked up, and realised that he was looking over my shoulder, at the laptop screen behind me.

A member of the computer support team, Frank had trouser hems hovering somewhere above his ankles, a check shirt covering a pigeon chest and a face that had been taken over by large black-rimmed glasses. He was the epitome of the IT geek.

"Hello Frank," I said, more loudly than I would normally speak, attempting to draw his attention to me, and away from my computer. At the same time, I scooted my chair back, so that my body would block the display. It also put some distance between me and Frank, who had an irritating habit of ignoring social mores regarding personal space.

Stubby fingers delved into his shirt pocket and pulled out a black tablet. He pushed the screen toward my face. "According to our records, you've downloaded some unauthorised software."

Resisting the impulse to check that Gremlin was still covered by the computer magazine I'd artfully placed at the side of my laptop, I shook my head. "I got something from the software library, that's all."

With a frown of irritation, he checked the tablet screen. "That's not what it says here."

"Let me see." I held out my hand for him to give me the device. What could I do to get rid of this idiot and back to my search results? I glanced at the display. "Yes. SmartNet. It's in the software library." I returned the gadget. "Go and check it yourself."

He planted his feet. "Show me." A finger waggled imperiously at my computer.

"Frank!" A sharp voice interrupted him.

We both turned, to see Nicholas facing us with his hands on his hips.

"Stop bothering Izzy. She's working on some data for me, and she's got a tight deadline." With a raised palm, he wiggled his fingers in the direction of the exit. "Let her get on with her work."

Frank jutted his jaw. "I just need—"

"No you don't." My boss pointed at the door again. "She

has my full authority, and if you delay her any further, I'll be reporting you to Pam." Pamela Emerson was Frank's boss.

With his tail between his legs, and muttering under his breath, Frank scuttled off.

"Thanks," I said, hoping that Nicholas wouldn't hang around, for he might see what was displayed on my screen. And had Frank seen it? It wouldn't make much sense if you didn't know about the issues I was investigating, but I was already suspicious of Nicholas.

Although... would he have defended me against Frank if he was the one doing the hacking? I smiled up at him and gave him a nod. Fortunately, he took the hint and strode away to his desk.

Mentally wiping my brow, I turned back to the laptop.

Someone had used 'RobinHood' to log in to a deposit account on one of our banking servers. I clicked onto the account details. Large sums of money—*exceedingly* large sums—came into and out of the account on a regular basis. The interest that accrued was significant and regularly withdrawn. But... there was something about the account that looked off.

It took me a minute to work out what was wrong, and then I sat up taller, my mouth open in disbelief.

"Izzy!" Nicholas' sharp voice called my name from a couple of desks down.

Suppressing a sigh of annoyance, I stood up and looked over the partitions. "Yes?"

"Can we go to meeting room two? I have the details of your bonus for this year."

The expression on his face was stony, and I didn't fancy my chances of arguing for another slot. "Okay," I said, inwardly groaning. "Be right there."

With a longing look at the interesting information on my laptop screen, I closed it down, so prying eyes wouldn't see what I was working on. After removing the Gremlin USB and looping the chain round my neck, I grabbed a notepad and pen, and followed him out of the office.

———

THE MEETING about my bonus was relatively short, and relatively unexciting. Rather than the five and six-figure sums I'd heard some of my longer-serving colleagues talk about in the past, this year I was to receive a relatively modest four-figure sum.

Being as I hadn't particularly expected it or relied on it, I was happy with that amount. It would be in my bank account by the new year, so I'd have a think between now and then about what I'd do with it.

It wasn't enough to make any significant purchase like a house or car, and not enough to be worth investing, so I would probably either spend or save. Or maybe a bit of both...

I was musing on that while I returned to the office. Nicholas had asked me to send Manda up next, and I was just passing my desk on the way to hers when something pulled me up short. My heart started to hammer in my chest.

Someone's been sitting on my chair. I felt like one of Goldilocks' three bears. The laptop screen, which I'd closed before I left the office, was sitting open, and my chair was facing the desk, when I'd left it facing outwards.

A chill ran down my spine. Was someone spying on me? Rounding the partition, I waved to get Manda's attention. She pulled off her headphones. "Hi Manda, Nicholas wants to see you in meeting room two. But, did you notice if anyone was at my desk in the last wee while?"

She waggled her head. "No, nobody that I saw."

"You sure? I left my computer closed, and now it's open."

She craned her neck to see over the divider. "Could be

you forgot," she said dismissively, then ostentatiously closed down her own computer, before gliding off to the meeting room.

I clenched my jaw. Who could have been at my desk? We weren't away that long. Trying to appear casual, I scanned the other desks around our pod. Nobody was paying any attention, and a lot of the seats were empty.

Nicholas was ruled out, I realised, since I'd been with him and left him upstairs before I came straight back. Between that fact and his intervention with Frank, I was starting to trust him again.

Could it have been Manda? She had a real brass neck if it was. And why would she? She always seemed too caught up in her own work—and her trashy gossip magazines—to be worried about mine.

Maybe Frank had come back and snooped, his jobsworth instincts compelling him to discover what was really on my computer? He was perhaps the most likely candidate.

Whoever it was, my hackles were up, and I couldn't let it go. Locking the laptop in my desk drawer, I hurried out of the open-plan area and down the stairs to the large Computer Support office where Frank worked. If it had been him, I had an idea of how to winkle that out.

The first section on the left was the noisy one, where a lone guy and two ladies clacked away at their keyboards as they talked nineteen to the dozen into their headset microphones. Those were our phone support IT staff, a thankless task, if you asked me. They had constant targets and no real letup in the barrage of questions and help requests that came in to them, every minute of every hour, from random members of the public.

In the middle of the area was a large, almost square arrangement of desks with so many monitors and computers on it that the owner could have used a different one each day of the week. It was Pamela Emerson's workspace, but she wasn't there right now.

There were some empty seats at the far end of the room. Possibly Pam was also having a series of meetings about bonuses with her staff. Maybe that's what the management briefing Nicholas had been at this morning was all about— how to break it gently to your team members that they were getting very little in their Christmas stocking from Santa Bleubank. I clenched my fists.

Beyond Pam's desk was the main computer support area. Grouped there were the technicians who installed and fixed the hardware and software used in Bleubank's London offices. I was making a beeline for Frank's desk when I caught sight of a strange—yet familiar—face, which drew me up short.

It was the guy from the café yesterday lunchtime, the one who'd been talking to Walter Oxley the CFO. What was he doing here?

Taking a minute to school my features into something other than surprise or anger, I pretended to study a leaflet on Pam's desk. Why would a mere computer tech be meeting a member of our board of directors for lunch? It seemed strange. Unless he wasn't a part of the support department? But then why would he be sitting here?

There was only one way to find out...

———

"Afternoon, guys," I said, then looked pointedly at Oxo's lunch date. "Is that you got a new team member?"

He stood up in a waft of lemony aftershave and held out a hand. "Lee Isaacson. I've been transferred from the Birmingham office." Gone was the suit from yesterday—presumably a first-day nerves thing—but he still appeared a little starchy in a blue shirt with all the buttons done up, a paisley-patterned golfing pullover and dark trousers with a crease down the front of each leg so sharp it could take your eye out.

I shook his hand. His grip was about as droopy as a daffodil after Easter, and I had to resist the desire to wipe my palm on the seat of my leggings. "I'm Izzy Paterson from the IT Security team. Nice to meet you," I said, pasting a fake smile on my face. "When did you start here?"

"Just arrived yesterday," he replied. I couldn't quite place his accent, but it wasn't Birmingham, for sure. His voice was over-loud, almost as if he was slightly deaf.

At the third desk was Charlie Thwaite. With her part-shaved, part-spiky hair, skinny jeans, fitted grey t-shirt and black leather jacket, she looked far too 'street' to be working in IT. She was the most relatable member of their team, and I was always glad if it was her who answered any call-outs on our floor. I resolved to get her alone when I could find a chance, and ask her along to Friday's karaoke night. It would be good to have some more girls there. But I didn't want straight-laced Frank to get wind of the event. He'd be sure to put a dampener on things.

"I actually came down to see Frank," I said, turning to face the bespectacled technician. Watching his face closely, I continued, "I remembered after you left the office earlier. I *did* install another app on my laptop—some spy software that records keystrokes and timestamps them." I was lying through my back teeth, but I was hoping the threat of being logged by this software might flush out the person who'd used my computer.

There was no reaction from Frank other than a flaring of his nostrils, but out of the corner of my eye I saw a flash of movement from Lee. I glanced over, but he'd dropped his head and was studying something on his phone.

Frank, meantime, was pushing a piece of paper at me across his desk. "Software installation record form. SIRF. Fill it in and return it to us." He fixed me with a beady eye. "Next time, complete the form first," he commanded.

I grabbed the paperwork and turned to leave, stealing one last peek at Lee before I went. He lifted his head and gave me a sideways look, his jaw jutting. I couldn't work out if he was annoyed at me for not sticking to the rules, or if there was something else going on.

From his reaction, it didn't seem that Frank would have been the one to snoop on my computer. Could it have been Lee? But why? He only started yesterday and would hardly have had time to use his *own* PC, let alone logging in to mine. And Frank was the one who'd been in our office earlier.

My feet dragged as I climbed the stairs. Who on earth was the baddie here? I seemed to have more clues than ever, but no idea who was hacking into our systems. Sadly, I was also clueless as to whether they were outsiders, or if it was an inside job.

However, I *did* now know what was going on.

Arriving back at our office, I seated myself at my desk and retrieved the laptop. Opening the lid, I stared at the figures on the screen before me.

Just before Nicholas had interrupted me, asking me to attend the bonus meeting, I'd worked out that the Robin Hood account I'd been looking at was being used as a temporary 'pass-through' account for large sums of foreign currency.

They'd be deposited in the account one day and transferred out the next. Nothing stayed in the account for any longer than twenty-four hours, which was very unusual. But that single day in a high-earning account was enough to amass significant amounts of interest.

It wasn't clear to me where the foreign currencies were coming from, but it mightn't matter. If only I could discover where that interest was being transferred to, perhaps I'd find our miscreant.

Flexing my fingers, I poised my hands above the keyboard, determined to discover who was receiving these large amounts of dosh. Was Robin Hood really taking from the rich to give to the poor, like in the legend? It was time to 'follow the money' and find out.

CHAPTER SEVEN

TWO HOURS LATER, I was just about tearing my hair out.

The interest from the Robin Hood pass-through account was withdrawn and transferred to another deposit account, where it would stay for a day. Then it was siphoned off from there into a different account, and so on, and on, like a daisy chain, accumulating further interest along the way.

It reminded me of the anonymous shell corporations that shady businessmen used to evade tax—or the law. But, perplexingly, these deposit accounts had no beneficiary information associated with them. Not even the main Robin Hood account had an owner's name linked to it. And unless I could find the payee's name, I wouldn't be able to work out who had set up this elaborate scheme.

All I could think was that the accounts had been generated electronically by a computer program, because to have been set up manually by the normal channels, an account would have a name and address associated with it.

So that narrowed my list of suspects to people who had computer programming skills. The number of Bleubank staff with a background in writing software was limited. But an external hacker could do something like that with their eyes closed and their hands tied behind their back.

Pulling out my secret project notebook, I was about to start noting down names, when I noticed the time. *Rats.* I'd need to get a wiggle on if I wanted to arrive home for six-thirty like I'd promised Trinity. My list of suspects would have to wait.

———

DESK TIDIED and laptop locked away, I grabbed my stuff and hurried across the office, out into the hall and then through the door to the back stairs.

With an exclamation of annoyance, I pulled up short. For some reason the lights were out, and the stairwell was in darkness. It was so black that I couldn't even see the banisters I knew must be just a few feet in front of me.

Pulling out my phone, I flicked to the torch app, clicked a few buttons, and, like magic, a circle of light illuminated the wall to either side of the doorway. In common with other horsey girls who often had to negotiate dark barns or paddocks, I was a regular user of the phone's flashlight function.

Aha! I spotted the light switch and pressed it down. But nothing happened.

Frowning, I tried again—with the same result, of course—then berated myself for stupidly expecting something to change. Presumably a fuse had blown, and that was why the lights were out.

I looked from the black stairs to the door behind me, and contemplated going the long way round to the main staircase. But, since I already had the torch out, laziness won, and I decided to find my way down in the dark. Surely if I could negotiate a dark, muddy field, I could manage a few stairs.

But I'd only taken two steps down the first flight when the beam of light from my phone glinted on something thin and silvery. I gasped, and my foot stopped, hovering in midair. Carefully, ever so carefully, I put it back down. Was that…?

Reaching down, I played the light along the length of the tread. There was an almost invisible wire, positioned exactly where, if I hadn't spotted it first, it would've tripped me and sent me flying down the flight of concrete steps.

Had some saboteur put it there deliberately? My blood ran cold. Surely you wouldn't do this accidentally? And, had it been meant for someone else, or for me? Feeling paranoid, I shone the torch beam around, then up and down the stairwell, making sure I was alone.

Taking a deep breath, I took a tight hold of the banister and stepped very carefully over the wire. My pulse thumping in my ears, I negotiated the rest of the stairs with extreme caution, but there didn't appear to be any further booby-traps.

When I reached the ground floor, I almost ran across to the reception desk and gabbled at the security guard. "You have to come." I gestured wildly behind me. "There's a trip wire on the stairs and I nearly fell. The lights are out. We have to stop anyone else from coming down there."

A stocky, middle-aged man with a foxy face and thinning hair, Harry McPhail was an ex-policeman with designs on an easier life for his last few years of work, and plans to retire to the South coast. To give him his due, even though I must've sounded like a total lunatic, he didn't try to have me committed. Instead, with raised eyebrows, he silently picked up his cap, reached under the desk for a torch, then walked around to join me.

"Lead on, Miss Paterson," he said, motioning toward the stairs, then pulled a radio out of his pocket. Pushing a black button on the top, he spoke into the handset. "Blue four to control. Investigating a report of an obstacle in our south-west stairwell." He it off and whispered to me. "Which floor?"

"Second."

Harry relayed that information, then pushed through the door to the stairs, with me following close behind. Reaching across, he flicked the light switch—and the lights came on!

My mouth hung open. "What?" I turned to him. "They were off a minute ago, I swear. I tried the switch on our landing."

His eyebrows raised again, then he shrugged. "Could be the switch is faulty." He jerked his chin up the stairs. "Show me where you saw this wire."

I led him up the dull grey steps until we reached the spot where I'd narrowly avoided breaking my neck. Except—there was nothing there. No tripwire, and no sign anything had *ever* been there. I gazed angrily around. Was someone playing tricks on me? But, as before, the stairwell was empty.

"It was here," I said, pointing across the step and indicating where the wire had been. "Three steps down. Honest it was. Tied round the metal railing on either side. It must have been moved."

Harry took off his peaked hat and scratched his head. "Now, Miss Paterson, I'm sure you're not one for flights of fancy. But, the facts are, the lights are working and there's nothing on the stairs." He gave me a level stare. "Could you have been mistaken?"

"I know what—" I stopped myself. I had been going to tell him that I knew what I saw. But there was no wire there now, and no evidence there ever had been. Berating myself for not taking a photo as proof, I sighed.

Voices approached the door above us, and a couple of staff members pushed through and clattered past down the stairs, wishing us a "Good night."

"Miss?" Harry prompted.

With a shake of my head, I took a step downwards. "Sorry to waste your time." My shoulders slumped. "I don't know what happened."

But as we descended, I grew more sure with every stride that someone—presumably the Robin Hood hacker—somehow knew that I was onto them. And, because of that, they'd tried to incapacitate me. Or worse.

My mouth went dry. Things were getting serious now.

———

STRAP-HANGING on my way home in the underground, the situation at work kept going round and round in my head.

The stations on my route passed in a blur of white tiles, crowded platforms and bright lights. Lost in my thoughts in the jam-packed compartment of the tube train, I swayed and rocked and bounced as the carriage barrelled along the metal rails, oblivious to the chatter of the surrounding travellers, and the smell of soot and humanity that pervaded the air in these underground vehicles.

What I kept coming back to was: if the tripwire really *had* been intended for me—and the fact that it disappeared as soon as I'd gone into the main concourse supported that—then it pointed to the Robin Hood hacker being someone on the inside. One of my colleagues in Bleubank, not an external perpetrator. Which narrowed the list of suspects considerably, but scared the pants off me.

The attempt to nobble me must mean that I was getting close to an answer. But how would the hacker know that I was making progress with the investigation?

And how did they know that I was leaving the office, timing it just right to set the wire and fuse the lights? I wasn't the only person who used the back stairs. Could they somehow be spying on *me*, the way I was snooping on them via the network sniffer? Or was it someone nearby, who'd spotted me putting my things away?

The thought that I was being observed so closely chilled my bones.

CHAPTER EIGHT

THE AROMA that met me when I entered my flat was indescribably amazing. And the wave of relief that washed over me when I realised that I was safely home was also rather surprising. I puffed out a big sigh and let my shoulders relax.

After dropping my bag on the floor by the door and hanging my coat, I hurried through to the kitchen. "Evening. That smells incredible!" I said, craning my neck to see into the steaming pot that Trinity was stirring on the stove. "What is it?"

"It's Jamaican black-eyed pea curry. And it's ready now," she replied with a smile.

"Oh wow. I can't wait, it looks delicious."

Trinity spooned fluffy white rice onto two plates, then topped it with the fragrant, creamy sauce.

From the first bite, I was in heaven. "Trinity, this must be the best veggie curry I've ever tasted. Where d'you learn to cook like that?"

"Well now, I'd have to thank my Jamaican grandmother. She loved to cook, and she taught my dad, and then me when I was just a little thing." She tucked a lock of her long, black hair behind her ear. "It was Dad did most of the cooking in our house. 'E said it relaxed him."

"Feel free to carry on the tradition," I said with a wink. Preparing food was *not* my favourite pastime. Eating, yes. But if it took longer than twenty minutes to cook, I wasn't interested.

Trinity laughed. "What're you like! But I don't mind cooking when I've got the time. I find it relaxing too. Now, tell me," she put her fork down and leaned on her elbows, looking intently over the table at me, "how d'you get on today? Did you find the hacker?"

I made a face. "Nearly. But he—or she—must know I'm onto them. There was a tripwire across the stair when I came out of the office tonight, and all the lights were out. It's lucky I noticed it."

"Seriously?" Her eyes turned to saucers. "What did the police say?"

Colour rose in my cheeks. "We didn't call them. I got the security guard, but by the time we got back up the stairs, the lights were working and the tripwire was gone. I'm not sure he believed me."

"Men!" Trinity slammed her fist down on the table. "Does it need you to get a broken neck before they take you seriously?"

"Hopefully not!" I tried to lighten the atmosphere. The male of the species obviously wasn't at the top of Trinity's Christmas Card list at this moment in time.

"You should tell your boss."

I tapped my fork against my bottom lip. "Actually, I think you're right. This is getting too much for me on my own. I'll tell him tomorrow. But now," I pointed at her half-full plate, "let's eat up so we can go and sort Dwayne out. That guy needs to know he can't mess with my friend!"

I HAD to admit to feeling a little nervous as we climbed the stairs to Dwayne's second-floor flat. A bulb was out on the first-floor landing, which had me clutching at my bag, wondering if I could use it as makeshift cudgel if need be. In heels, tights and a business suit, I felt like an actor playing a part. Which I guess I was.

Someone had been cooking cabbage, and the metallic smell hung in the still air like a bizarre chemical weapon. In a flat down the corridor, another resident was murdering a cat. No, wait... they were practicing scales on a violin. The RSPCA could stand down.

Trinity stopped outside a dented white door. "Ready?" she asked.

Smoothing down my skirt, I took a deep breath. "Yep. Let's go for it."

She leaned on the rusty doorbell, and, somewhere inside the flat, tinny Westminster chimes announced our arrival. Half a minute later, Dwayne threw the door open with a belligerent, "Yeah?" before he even saw who was there.

I stepped forward, my heels clicking on the concrete hallway. "Dwayne Brooks? Dwayne Jeffrey Brooks?"

He crossed his arms and leaned against the doorjamb, just like he had in Jasmin's photo. "Yeah. What's it to you?" With a baseball cap crammed over his short black hair, three gold chains hanging around his neck, and the crotch of his trousers drooping somewhere around his knees, Dwayne looked like an extra in a rap video.

"I'm Isobel Paterson of Paterson, Paterson and Banks. I'm here on behalf of my client, Ms Trinity Allen." I swivelled my eyes over my shoulder at Trinity, then pulled a piece of letterhead paper—for my fictional company of lawyers, concocted this lunchtime—out of my bag and thrust it at him. "This is a cease and desist letter, ordering you to stop harassing my client for rental monies."

He shoved it back at me. "You can go take a hike."

Holding up my hands, I refused to accept the letter from him. "We have evidence that, firstly, you are contravening the rules of your tenancy by sub-letting to another party, and secondly, that you have already replaced my client with another tenant, namely one Jasmin Freeman, and therefore Ms Allen now owes no rent."

Pointing a finger at my face, Dwayne started to bluster, "But, but—"

I cut him off. "Should you bother my client again, we will be forced to inform your landlord of the illegal sub-let." Signalling that our meeting was at an end, I clicked shut the catch on my shoulder bag. My frosty smile didn't reach my eyes. "Good evening, Mr Brooks." Then I turned on my heel and marched off down the corridor, followed quickly by Trinity.

We were almost at the bottom of the stairs when I could hold it in no longer. Leaning back against the wall, I let the laughter loose. "His face!" I cried, tears running down my cheeks.

Trinity was holding her sides. "Priceless, it was. Priceless! You should join the Royal Shakespeare, Izzy. That were some performance!"

Fishing a tissue from my pocket, I wiped my eyes. "Hopefully that's the last you'll see of him."

"An' good riddance too!"

———

ON THE WAY HOME, Trinity and I stopped off to buy some celebratory ice cream. It seemed counterintuitive, since the weather was on the frosty side of normal, but we passed the drive-through outlet and both had a hankering at the same time. The plan was to make some hot chocolate, put our feet up in front of an episode of CSI, and gorge ourselves on delicious creamy dessert.

You know what they say about the best-laid plans…

As I turned the car through the short brick pillars flanking the entrance to my apartment building, I jammed on the brakes, gasping in surprise. Before us in the car park were crowds of people, a red fire engine with its blue lights flashing, and beside that a white plumber's van.

My pulse hammering, I craned my neck, looking for the fire. Or smoke. But I couldn't see any. There was just a throng of residents flanked by brown-uniformed firefighters wearing yellow helmets.

In the passenger seat beside me, Trinity was also gaping out of the window. "What's going on?" she asked, just as a dark-haired, chunky fireman strode toward us and motioned for me to roll down the window.

He leaned in to speak to us. "Evening, miss." He noticed Trinity and inclined his head at her, an appreciative glint in his eye. "Ladies, sorry. May I ask why you're visiting here this evening?" His breath smelled of peppermint and his voice sounded like chocolate.

"I'm not visiting. I live here."

"Ah." A radio crackled in Officer After-dinner-mint's top pocket, and he pulled it out and frowned at it. Then he turned back to me. "Which flat?"

"Two C."

"Ah." This time the simple word carried layers of meaning. My heart sank.

"Is something wrong, Officer?"

He tilted his head at a parking space near the road. "Park your car over there, and I'll get the super to have a word with you." He moved away and started speaking into the radio handset.

Starting the car again, I glanced over at Trinity. Her face was tight, her normally smiling mouth set in a line of concern. "I've not got a good feeling about this," I said.

"Neither have I."

With a growing sense of dread, we got out of the car and headed toward the entrance. I sniffed the air, but couldn't smell smoke. This was a weird fire. If that's what it was...

We were met by another fireman, this time a taller guy with a silver stripe on his collar, grey goatee and light blue eyes. "Ladies," he greeted us, "Officer Yourdis tells me you live in apartment two C."

I nodded, scared that if I spoke my voice would come out in a squeak.

"And your landlord is Mr Bashir Noorzai?"

"Yes." Yep, I was right. I sounded like a mouse.

He sucked air through his teeth. Beside me I thought I heard Trinity whimper. Officer Yourdis hovered on the edge of the crowd in front of us, looking concerned.

"Has the flat burned down?" I asked, running through a mental checklist to try and think if we'd left any appliances on, or left something flammable next to a heater. But nothing came to mind. We'd not been home for long that evening, just enough time for dinner and then quickly getting changed before we went to Dwayne's.

"No," his chin jerked up. "Not that. But your neighbour in the flat above has gone on holiday."

"Yes. The Steadmans."

"The same." He hooked a gloved thumb around the flash-light strapped below his right shoulder. "Unfortunately, they left a tap dripping in their bath, and the stopper was in. It overflowed this evening and took down part of the ceiling in your flat."

"Oh no!" My hand flew to my mouth.

Out of the corner of my eye, I saw Trinity start to sway. Before I could grab her, Officer Yourdis was there, propping her up and guiding her over to a bench at the entrance to the communal garden.

I had to leave my friend in the care of the firefighter, because at that moment I was confronted by my landlord, Mr Noorzai, all waving hands and rolling eyes and effusive apologies.

"Miss Paterson, Miss Paterson," he said, almost bowing before me, "it is so terrible what has happened, so terrible. I am so sorry. So very sorry. But," he raised a hand and smiled at me, showing a row of impossibly white teeth, "I have a proposition to make. A proposition for you."

I blinked. I hadn't been propositioned by a man for a long time. A *very* long time. Even one in a shiny brown suit, slip-on shoes and thin moustache.

"On the top floor," Mr Noorzai continued, "I have a flat for rent. A most lovely apartment. Fully furnished, with the two bedrooms, a bathroom with shower, and a kitchen with the built-in oven. Most excellent."

"That's good," I replied, not quite sure what he was expecting me to say.

"For you," he said, looking pleased with himself.

"For me?" I repeated, frowning.

"Yes. You must take that flat, you can live there most comfortably while the builders repair your place. For no extra charge."

"No extra charge?" I repeated again, my eyebrows climbing my forehead.

"Yes, no extra. Until your place is ready. Just continue the bank payment every first of the month as you do now."

I flicked my eyes at the bearded firefighter, who was still beside me. He lifted his shoulders.

"Uh, okay," I said to my landlord, hardly believing my luck. A two-bedroom flat in London would usually cost a good few hundred extra pounds per month. Maybe several hundred. "Thank you. But," I glanced across at Trinity, who was sitting on the wooden bench, being ministered to by the younger fireman, "is it all right if I have a friend to stay with me? She's between places right now and had to move out at short notice."

Mr Noorzai followed my gaze. "Of course, of course. And," his mouth curved into a smile, "if you should both be deciding to continue on in the top-floor flat, I might perhaps maybe be persuaded to give you a most generous deal on the rental." I could almost see the pound signs scrolling before his eyes. Fishing in his pocket, he produced a keyring, placing it in my hand with a flourish.

"Great. Thanks, Mr Noorzai. We'll get moved in then."

I turned to the firefighter. "Are we able to get our things from the flat?"

He held up a finger, then said something unintelligible into his radio. A crackly voice seemed to reply in the affirmative, because he nodded at me. His eyes swung to the garden bench. "I'll get Officer Yourdis to accompany you and make sure everything is safe."

When we were finally installed in the new flat, I was almost falling asleep on my feet, and Trinity had a dinner date with a handsome firefighter on Thursday evening.

Leaning against the front door, I surveyed my new domain. Similar in layout to my old flat, it was just a little bigger all over—plus it had a second bedroom, so Trinity didn't need to sleep on the couch.

Everything was white or grey, with an accent wall in the lounge area which was decorated in a warm plum shade. Overall, the effect was quite restful. "I could get used to this,"

I said to Trinity, who had fallen into the grey leather couch with a sigh of contentment.

"I'm trying not to," she said, swivelling her feet back onto the floor and twisting round to look at me. "I'll need to start flat-hunting again tomorrow."

Pursing my lips, I stared at her for a moment.

"What?" she asked, looking alarmed.

"What if..." I was thinking aloud, which was not my normal modus operandi, being more of a planner. "What if we stayed on here? We've got the first month effectively for free. There are two bedrooms. You could save yourself a lot of hassle and move in here. With me. Then you don't have to find another place."

She scrunched her nose and waved an arm round the room. "Someone like me couldn't ever afford somewhere like this. It's way above my pay grade."

"Hmmm." I went over to the dining table, where my computer stuff had been placed, temporarily, and switched on my laptop. A minute later, I'd found Mr Noorzai's advert for the flat. Like I'd thought, it was a chunk more expensive than the one downstairs. "How much were you paying at Dwayne's?" I asked.

When she told me, I did a quick calculation. "If you could afford to keep paying that, we could both stay here, and I'd actually save a little each month."

"Are you serious?" Her face brightened.

"Yeah. We could share the cooking, share the bills—that will probably make things even cheaper for both of us."

She came to look over my shoulder at the advert. "Oh, I can't have that. You'd be paying more than me. That's not fair."

"It's fine. It's less than I'm paying right now, and this is a nicer place."

She still didn't look convinced.

"Tell you what," I said, stifling a yawn, "since it's all paid for, let's give it to the end of the month." I shut the laptop down. "Or at least till I go home for Christmas. We can see how we're getting along, and how we like it here in the daylight, and then decide."

My yawn must've been infectious, because Trinity couldn't speak for a minute. She just bobbed her head, then mumbled. "Okay. Deal!"

Sleepily, I stumbled to my new bedroom, passing the forlorn tub of ice-cream melting quietly on the kitchen counter. I shook my head. This evening definitely hadn't gone the way I'd expected.

CHAPTER NINE

As soon as I arrived at work the next morning, I dumped my bag at my desk and made a beeline for Nicholas. "Can I get a word with you?" I asked.

He looked up at me over his glasses, frowning. I could see the annoyance in his face, but something in my demeanour must've changed his mind, because his expression altered to one of concern. He grabbed his tablet and stood. "Let's go and see if there's a meeting room free."

Five minutes later, I'd told him the story of the tripwire and the intruder on my computer, and he appeared even more grave. "This all happened yesterday afternoon, you say?"

"Yes."

If he'd pressed his lips together any harder, they'd have disappeared. "Devlin was away all day at that conference, wasn't he?" Nicholas asked, rhetorically.

I nodded.

He picked up the grey phone in the middle of the table and dialled Dev's extension. "Devlin," he barked, "join us in meeting room three." Putting the handset down, he turned to me. "It can't have been Devlin, since he wasn't here."

"That's what I thought too. Rules him out." A smile flickered on my lips. I was glad it wasn't my friend. "And it probably rules out external hackers too."

"Which means someone internal." Nicholas' eyes narrowed, and his long fingers drummed on the table, as if he was going through a list of our colleagues in his head, just like I had yesterday.

When he walked in a minute later, Dev's eyes widened when he saw me. "Morning," he said, then pulled out the chair opposite Nicholas.

Our boss took his glasses off and put them down. "Devlin, Izzy has been working on a special project for me."

"The annual report, yes." Dev leaned back, glancing from one of us to the other.

Nicholas scratched his beard. "It's a little more than that." He glanced across at me. "And now it's got somewhat more... complicated. I need you to double-team on this. Literally. Izzy isn't to go anywhere alone—you'll go to lunch together, and please can you see her to the station after work."

"What about the toilet?" Dev asked, obviously thinking this was some kind of joke.

"You can wait outside. And if she takes longer than five minutes, you phone security."

Dev looked from one of us to the other. "Seriously?"

"Deadly serious." Nicholas stood up, abruptly. "Izzy, you can fill Devlin in on the details. Two heads should be better than one. Maybe you can get this solved today, and we can all stop worrying."

The door slammed behind him, and Dev turned to me, his mouth open. "What's going on?"

"Let's go get a coffee. Caffè Fiorio. I need some caffeine, and I think we need to get out of the office for me to tell you the story."

———

DEV PUT down his china cup with a thump and stared at me, his eyes like saucers. "You're never serious?" A couple of people in the café turned to look at him, and he lowered his voice somewhat before he carried on. "There's someone at work stealing money from our systems and now they've tried to kill you?"

My hand shook a little as I put down my own cup. "I suppose... I hadn't thought of it in as stark terms as that, but, yes, that about sums it up."

He banged his fist on the table and swore. Quietly. "We need to get them, Izzy, before they get us." Green eyes caught mine. "Did you make a list of suspects yet?"

"Only in my head."

"Okay, let's start with that. We need to know who we're dealing with."

Somehow, it made me feel better that he was saying 'we'. The task of finding the hacker had seemed quite daunting when I was on my own, especially when there were so few clues. But with two of us on the job, surely we'd crack the case really quickly? It had to be easier... didn't it?

———

ON OUR WAY back to the office, we passed a newspaper stand, and one of the headlines caught my eye. I stopped abruptly, which caused Dev to almost crash into me. "Look." I pointed.

'Bleubank profits slump', the sandwich board declared. 'Investors nervous.'

My heart thumping, I turned to Dev. "We need to find this hacker, or none of us will have jobs come the new year."

I half expected him to argue, but for once he was silent, staring moodily at the newspapers in the kiosk. "You're right," he said after some moments. "This is serious."

We were both in a sombre mood when we got back to the office. The first thing I did was to scout around for a hidden spy camera, or something that would explain how the hacker knew my movements. But we didn't want them to know we were onto them, so I disguised my search by making it look like I was dusting my shelves and rearranging the items on my desk.

After polishing everything that didn't move, and possibly even a few things that did, I had found nothing. "Fancy a cup of tea?" I asked Dev, raising my eyebrows, so he'd know I wanted to talk—without being overheard.

He stood up with alacrity and grabbed his mug. "Sure thing."

I led the way to the kitchen area at the other end of the open-plan office. When we got there, two co-workers were in the process of making coffee, so Dev and I made small talk until they'd left.

When we had the place to ourselves, he filled the kettle and started it boiling. "So, did you find anything?" he asked, while he got his mug out of the cupboard.

"Nope. There's nothing on my desk. Unless I'm totally blind."

Dev stared intently at my eyes for a moment as if he was checking, then laughed when he saw my expression. "Gotcha!" he said. Then he leaned back against the counter so that he had a good view of the office. "Don't point," he said, "in case they're watching. But what about the book-shelves between our desks and the web team?"

Picking up my cup as if cradling a coffee, I went to stand beside him. "I see what you mean. That would give a perfect line of sight." I sighed. "But I won't get away with dusting there."

"No, probably you wouldn't." The kettle clicked off behind us, and Dev busied himself making his tea. "I could hunt for a book, though."

"True. And if it's not there?" I got my coffee things down from the cupboard.

"We can talk about it at lunchtime. Where d'you want to go? Caffè Fiorio again?"

"Just somewhere to get a sandwich. I can't afford to eat there every day."

"Tell me about it! Especially if the bonuses are to be low this year."

"They are. Did you have your meeting with the boss man yet?"

He shook his head. "With me being out of the office yesterday and then what's been going on this morning, there hasn't been a chance." He frowned at me. "How's that going to work, if I'm babysitting you?"

"You're not babysitting me," I said, pushing his arm. "You're working with me."

"Tomah-to, tomay-to," he said, with a wink. "Whatever."

I gave him some stink-eye, then thought for a minute. "I could go and visit Charlie in Computer Support. I wanted to ask her to the karaoke night without the guys overhearing. You could meet me there after."

"Okay, I'll speak to Nick when we get back and work something out." He gazed across the office again. "As for the spy cam, if I find anything, I'll call you over and ask if you know if there's a more recent edition of this book. If I don't, you'll know I drew a blank."

Dev didn't find anything.

———

WE RECONVENED AT LUNCHTIME. At a tiny, brightly painted shop owned by an industrious Polish man who insisted in calling me 'Madam' and Dev, 'Sir', we bought our sandwiches .

Then we took them to a park bench outside a medieval church down a narrow side street a block away from the office. With walls made from irregular ancient stones, two wide stained glass windows above two solid wooden doors, and a small clock tower peeking above the roof, it was an intriguing building. Why two doors? One of these days I'd need to explore inside and find the answer.

Above our heads, a breeze rustled the leaves of an old oak tree. It also brought the scent of garlic from a nearby Italian restaurant. Dev's stomach rumbled, and I sneezed.

"Bless you," Dev said, automatically.

A bandy-legged grey-haired man shuffled down the steps from the church, turning his hat in his hands. The creases on his face and the stoop of his back made him look like he carried the cares of the world. I had an idea of how he felt.

"So," said Dev, taking a bite from his chicken sandwich. "What do we do now?"

Watching the old man shamble along the pavement, I pulled out my falafel wrap, and thought about the audiobook mystery I was listening to on my commute to work. "Hamish Macbeth always seems to investigate the backgrounds of his suspects, and he gets clues that way."

Dev looked at me like I'd grown an extra head. "Hamish who?"

I waved a hand dismissively. "He's a policeman in a mystery series. But you're missing the point. If we check out our suspects' backgrounds and find out who's got programming skills, we can see who might have been able to set up those shell accounts. Or we could go from the other end, see if anyone is spending lots of money—new car, new house, whatever."

Chewing on his sandwich, Dev's head bobbed slightly. "You might have something there. But... should we not keep following the trail of the bank accounts? It sounded like you'd got close to the last of them."

"That's true." We both ate in silence for some time while we mulled things over. "How about I carry on with the accounts, and you start investigating the list of suspects?"

Dev wrinkled his nose. "If I'm honest, I think you'd be better doing the social media stuff. Have you seen my Face-Book profile?"

I hadn't. But a few taps on my phone screen later, I was looking at an anonymous grey icon. "Looks just like you," I teased.

"Ha, ha," he said mirthlessly, taking a swig from the bottle of water he'd bought with his sandwich.

"What about Twitter? D'you do that?"

"Not me. I can't be bothered with all that phoney stuff, people trying to make their lives sound exciting." He looked sideways at me. "I prefer face-to-face. Real people."

I swallowed. The conversation seemed to be venturing into dangerous territory again. "Okay," I said brightly, "You follow the money, I'll spy on our colleagues."

There was a beat of silence. A muscle jumped in Dev's cheek. Then he said, "Talking about that, we still need to work out how the hacker knew you were leaving last night."

"Yeah. Maybe *they're* tracking the network, and they saw me logging out?"

"It could be. I'll look and see if there's a way to identify network scanners, check if anyone else is doing it apart from you."

I hesitated for a second, then blurted out, "There's something I need to tell you." My 'follow the money' comment had reminded me of the Secret Santa poem.

He stiffened.

"There's someone else who knows about the hacker. Apart from Nicholas, I mean. And Antoine."

Dev deflated a little. "Antoine?"

"In the Paris office. They were the first to notice the irregularities in the network. Anyway," I raised a hand impatiently, "at the Christmas party, my Secret Santa gave me a rhyme. A clue. That's how I knew to look for Robin Hood."

"Oh-kay." His forehead creased. "How come you never said at the time?"

"The rhyme said to keep it a secret."

"And you're telling me now because...?"

"Because you're off the suspect list."

He clutched his chest theatrically. "Moi?"

"I couldn't be sure. Until the tripwire thing. You were at that conference that day. So we figured you were innocent."

"We?"

"Me and Nicholas." I turned my palm up. "I suspected him, too, for a while."

"My, but you're the mistrustful one. So he's in the clear now?"

"He was out of the office when someone logged in to my computer."

Dev breathed out slowly. "Right. But Manda was there."

"In body. She had her headphones on, so she saw nothing. Or so she said."

"Hmm." Dev scratched at his designer stubble. "So, what do you think? Has she been taking out shares in 'Hello' magazine recently? Or buying her boots from Jimmy Choo?"

"Not that I've noticed."

He scrunched up his sandwich wrapper and dusted crumbs from his trousers. "Still, might as well start somewhere."

It felt yucky, investigating my colleagues. But Dev was

right. We had to start somewhere. I just hoped we weren't stirring up a hornet's nest.

CHAPTER TEN

WHEN WE GOT BACK to the office, Nicholas wanted to meet with Dev about his bonus, so I phoned down to Charlie Thwaite in Computer Support and arranged to visit her.

My minder—Dev—parted ways with me outside their door. "I'll come and find you after my meeting. Stay with Charlie till then."

"Yes, Sir!" I clicked my heels together and saluted him.

His eye roll would've made a great internet gif, if only I'd had my phone out in time to video him. I resolved to catch him at it some day, then pushed into the support department's office.

Charlie waved when she saw me. "How's it going?"

I made a face. "Long story. What about you?"

"Fine." She picked up two mugs from her desk. "Let's go get a drink."

Charlie led me over to their kitchen area. It had a similar layout to ours, but there were shouty notes posted on the fridge and cupboard doors reminding colleagues to 'clean up after yourselves' and 'if you didn't bring it, don't take it'. I had an idea who the passive-aggressive note poster was. "Frank's handiwork?" I asked Charlie, pointing at the post-its adorning the refrigerator.

She snorted. "How d'you guess?"

A few minutes later we both had coffees, and I'd told Charlie about the karaoke night on Friday. "Want to come?" I asked.

"Will Dev be there?"

I blinked at her, my mouth falling open. "Dev? But he's—"

"I know, he doesn't look like my type. But I think he's cute. And funny. He reminds me of Chris O'Dowd."

"From *The IT Crowd?*"

"Yep."

Now that she'd said it, I couldn't get it out of my head. They weren't quite doppelgangers, but they *could* be distant cousins. "I'd never have guessed. Is that why you come to our floor so often when things need fixed?"

She held up her hands. "What can I say?"

"Well, Friday night was his idea, so I think it's safe to assume he'll be there."

"Friday night?" said a loud voice behind us.

"Oh, hi Lee." Charlie tilted her head at me. "Izzy's team Christmas night out," she lied.

"Really. Where you going?" He shuffled past us, all starched shirt and lemon aftershave, then reached into the fridge, pulling out a can of coke.

"A pub," I answered. "Nowhere special."

He waggled his eyebrows. "A pub is *always* special."

"Lee," Charlie made a shoo-ing motion with her hand, "we're having a girly chat here, and you're short an X chromosome."

Muttering under his breath, he sloped off.

Charlie shook her head. "He's only been here three days, and he's already getting on my wick."

"What's his story?" I asked, thinking that I could kill two birds with one stone, and do some information gathering on the new start while chatting with my friend.

She wrinkled her nose. "Silver spoon, if you ask me. Mr Oxley is his step-dad, and he got the job without so much as an interview. Although, to be fair, he knows his stuff. He's just a bit loud and obnoxious with it."

"Ah!" Light dawned. "That explains why we saw him having lunch with Oxo on Monday."

Charlie shrugged. "Probably."

"So what does he do when he's not at work?"

"Irons his shirts, most likely," she said sarcastically. "I dunno. We've not chatted much."

I didn't dare ask any more, in case she thought my interest in Lee was more than professional, and was about to change the subject, when Dev appeared round the corner. Beside me, Charlie sucked in a breath.

Catching my eye, he jerked his chin at the ceiling. "Nick wants you for a meeting."

I feigned surprise. "Oh, okay." Stepping over to the sink, I emptied the dregs from my mug and rinsed it under the tap. "Thanks for the coffee, Charlie." I winked at her. "See you on Friday."

———

QUIETLY OPENING the door of the gym at the Community Centre, I tiptoed along the back of the room and found a space to unroll my exercise mat.

I was late, courtesy of a signalling fault on the District Line. Before I copied the rest of the class and lay down, I made a 'sorry' face to the Pilates teacher.

Queenie, a statuesque black woman in figure-hugging turquoise lycra, was at the front, helping another client with their double leg stretch. She gave me a thumbs-up and then announced the next move to the class.

For an hour I contorted my body and flexed my limbs in an effort to build control in my 'core'—the muscles in my mid-section.

Although I quite enjoyed the classes, I didn't do pilates solely for fun, but also to help with my horse riding. I'd realised a couple of years ago that the better balanced and controlled my body was in the saddle, the better Leo performed for me. So really, the pilates was cross-training for my dressage.

However, another benefit to the class was that it gave me time to think, and tonight's topic was the Robin Hood mystery.

Unfortunately, we'd got little further that afternoon. Dev had hit a brick wall tracing the deposit accounts, when he'd discovered that the next link in the chain was an account at a different bank. It wasn't impossible for him to trace, but it was a *lot* harder than finding information within Bleubank.

And I'd had no luck either. After hours spent surfing people's FaceBook profiles, hunting for evidence of extravagant spending, my eyes felt like they were crossing. But I'd found nothing. Could it be that we were looking at the wrong people? Or was the miscreant a master at hiding their tracks?

However, I wasn't done there. There were still the other social media channels to try. So that would be tomorrow's job.

I was just deciding where to start, when the door of the room burst open, and the janitor came clomping in. "Miss Queenie," he cried.

Everyone's heads turned to the back, then to Queenie at the front, like the spectators at a Wimbledon tennis match. "Yes, Eric?" Her voice was deep and melodious.

"You'll 'ave to stop the class, miss, I'm sorry." Murmurs of protest broke out at this pronouncement. "We're 'aving problems with the plumbing again, an' I'm going to 'ave to shut the place before we get flooded." He swiped a hand across his bald head.

Queenie clapped her hands. "Ladies! You can all practice your spine flexes and your scissor holds at home. We were almost finished with tonight's class, anyway. So let's stand and do one forward fold before we go, to stretch out our bodies, ready for the days ahead."

Dutifully, we all clambered to our feet and reached our fingers towards our toes. The grumbling died down as we all concentrated on lengthening our backs.

"I shall see you all next week!" Queenie's voice was bright as she sent us on our way. Unfortunately, her optimism would prove ill-founded.

———

IT WAS STILL DARK when I arrived at the livery yard early on Thursday morning. A sheen of rain made the street lights sparkle like diamonds and the tarmac glistened like anthracite. Away from the main road, tall trees absorbed the traffic noise, and it was relatively quiet in the car park when I got out of my Corsa.

Inside the barn, however, was a hive of activity. Obviously, I wasn't the only one who planned on riding before work. Straw flew in the air, horses nickered in anticipation of their breakfast feed, and people chatted briefly before scurrying off to complete their tasks.

With my saddle over my arm, I was returning to my stable and wondering whether I'd have time to clean the saddle after I finished, when Veronica Rothwell hustled across the barn. Veronica was the American lady whose horse had the stable opposite Leo.

"Izzy, dear," she said, touching my elbow and looking at me intently, "I need your help."

On the wrong side of forty, Veronica had one of those timeless faces that belied her age, and, even at this time of the morning, she somehow managed to look immaculate. With caramel-streaked hair cut in a sleek bob, an expensive quilted jacket and spotless beige jodhpurs, next to her I felt like a scruff. Then a waft of her Calvin Klein perfume made me sneeze.

"Excuse me," I said, then deposited my saddle over Leo's half-door and found a tissue in my pocket. "Sorry about that. What's up?"

"It's... you see... well, I heard, I heard you can find things out. About people. On FaceBook and suchlike."

I sighed inwardly. Trinity must've been talking. "Uh, perhaps. Tell me more?"

"Well, it's a trifle delicate..."

Giving her an encouraging smile, I reassured her. "Don't worry, I won't tell anyone." But I hoped she'd tell *me* in the next few minutes. I was on a schedule here, and if I wasn't in the saddle soon, I'd not have time to ride properly.

She pursed her lips. "It's like this. I met someone. A man. On Tinder. You know, the swipe left, swipe right app?"

I nodded. I'd heard of it, just never had the inclination to use it.

"He seems like a lovely person—very caring, very intelligent—but I'm..." she cast her eyes down, as if searching for the right word, "There's something about him... I'm not sure. I guess I'm worried he's interested in me for the wrong reasons."

My brow scrunched. "Why would that be?"

"Well, for my money of course." She brushed an imaginary hair off her jacket. "After I lost my second husband, I—Well, let's just say, I've got a gold card and I know how to use it." She looked up at me again, her expression hopeful. "But Kenneth, well, I wonder if he might be number three. I just need to be sure about him. You understand?"

Something tickled at the back of my nose, and I had to turn away so I didn't sneeze all over her. "Sorry," I said, my eyes watering. "Uh, yes. But wouldn't you be better with a private investigator?"

"Oh, I might. But I don't want someone following him around the place. He may spot them." She put her hand over mine, briefly. "You would be *much* more discreet, darlin', I'm sure. Check him out for me, see if he is what he says he is."

With a sweet smile, she added, "And of course I'd pay you for your time. I've heard these PIs charge one hundred pounds per hour. Would that be sufficient?"

It took a lot of effort to stop my jaw dropping. If that really *was* the going rate for detective work, maybe I should think seriously about starting 'Izzy Investigates' after all. In the bank, I'd need to be promoted to the Board of Directors to earn that sort of money.

"Um, do you have a timescale in mind? It's just," I scuffed my boot on the concrete, "I'm pretty busy at the office just now and I've got a dressage competition next weekend with Leo. So I'm not sure how much spare time I'll have. I don't want to let you down."

"Well, it would be nice to have an answer before Christmas—he's asked me to go away with him to a country hotel," she added in a hushed voice. "But really, anything at all that you can find for me would be just wonderful."

I swallowed. "I'll see what I can do." I motioned towards my stable. "Leave me a note of your phone number and his details, and I'll get it once I've ridden." I told her the information I needed about Kenneth, then checked my watch.

The conversation with Vivienne had knocked me behind schedule, and I *really* had to get going, so I'd have time to work on my dressage.

Tack cleaning would have to wait.

CHAPTER ELEVEN

THURSDAY'S INVESTIGATIONS at work were almost as frustrating as Wednesday's. When it got to five o'clock, Dev plonked himself on a clear piece of desk in my workspace, and we had a pow-wow.

He had worked out which bank the Robin Hood money was going to—a small, privately owned bank in Switzerland—but, to find out more, he would basically have to hack into their systems. This was exactly the thing he was trying to prevent in his current job at Bleubank. So, if they had staff anywhere near as good as him, it would prove impossible.

"But you never know," he said, ever the optimist. "Their security might not be on par with ours. After all," he raised a cheeky eyebrow, "they haven't got *me* working for them."

"Let me scratch your head for you," I said, holding up my fingers. I was about ten feet away from him, but I reckoned his head was at least that big.

For my part, I was still trawling through social media, and had seen more photos of babies and cats than one person needed for a lifetime. It was enough to make my forehead feel like someone was squeezing it in a vice. But I hadn't yet found anyone buying luxurious yachts, dripping with diamonds or jetting off on expensive holidays.

"Perhaps I need to look somewhere else," I suggested, as I rooted in my bag for painkillers. "I'm searching for the results of their ill-gotten gains. Maybe I should try to narrow it down, and find out who's got the appropriate computer skills to do this in the first place."

Dev rubbed his chin. "You may be right. There's no point flogging a dead horse." His eyes widened when he saw my face. "Sorry, rotten choice of words. There's no point banging your head against a brick wall," he amended. "If you're getting nowhere, maybe now's time to try something new."

Taking a gulp from my water bottle, I swallowed two tablets. "So, I need to hack into our personnel files, d'you think?" The idea of that was almost as icky as snooping on people's social media.

He screwed up his nose. "It seems to me that a quick search there for degrees in computer science might save us both a lot of time and hassle."

"Have you any idea how well secured the Human Resources database is?"

"I'm sure it's pretty old—pre-Y2K technology. So probably not that good."

"Okay. I'll have a look at that tomorrow." I looked up at him. "Time to call it a night?"

"Sure," he said, swinging his legs off the desk he'd been sitting on. "I'll just go get my jacket."

Fifteen minutes later, Dev was waving me off outside Monument tube station, on his way to the Bank station where he'd catch the Docklands Light Railway to his shared flat on the Isle of Dogs.

Pushing through the barriers, I made my way down to the District Line platform. It was the height of rush hour, and everywhere was crowded and noisy.

With a whoosh of warm, smelly air, a Circle Line train arrived. Almost as one, the throng of commuters pushed forward and into the domed carriages with their sliding doors. I kept to the side, but with more people arriving every second, the platform quickly filled again and I found myself near the front.

A glance at the information board told me that my train would arrive in two minutes. *Time for some Hamish Macbeth.* With the station this busy, I reckoned I was bound to be standing for most of the journey.

From my pocket, I produced my earbuds and pushed them into my ears. It dulled the surrounding noises, but I'd wait till I was in the carriage to switch the audiobook on, so I'd be certain to hear the train coming.

Sure enough, a minute later, lights appeared in the tunnel entrance, and I stepped forward, preparing to board my train. But suddenly, something pushed me from behind—hard. Hard enough to force me to the very edge of the platform.

Dimly, I heard the crowd behind me gasp, as I teetered on the concrete lip above the tracks, illuminated in the head-lights of the approaching train.

Throwing out my hands for balance, I tightened the core muscles I'd been working on at Pilates last night, and threw my weight backwards.

Just in the nick of time.

The engine of the tube train missed my nose by inches. Someone grabbed my arm, and someone else hauled on the back of my coat, and somehow I was standing there, upright, not lying splattered on the rails beneath.

"Are you okay?", "What happened?", "That were a near miss!" Voices filled the air, but I was still in action mode; reaction had not yet set in.

I spun around, searching the crowd behind me for anyone —or anything—suspicious. It was so busy that it was hard to be certain, but I was sure that I glimpsed a black-clad figure pushing through the mass of bodies and heading back toward the stairs. Was that my attacker? Or had it just been an accident? My brain was spinning.

Someone took my arm and led me into the carriage. Magically, a seat was free, and they ushered me onto it. "Are you all right, miss?" asked a young chap in an Arsenal top.

Nodding, I put my head in my hands and puffed out a loud breath. My heart was hammering, and I didn't trust myself to speak yet. But a question kept running through my brain.

Had I just been in the wrong place at the wrong time, or had Robin Hood tried to kill me once again?

———

RATHER THAN WALKING from the station as I usually would, I decided to take a taxi to the stables to collect my car. It was an expense I generally avoided, but tonight it seemed prudent. I didn't think that my attacker—if that's what it had been—had followed me, but I couldn't be one hundred percent sure.

As I paid the driver, I saw with relief that there were other cars in the car park. I wouldn't be alone here. The headache that had been brewing all afternoon had come back, and my eyes felt like they were being squeezed together. My throat had got in on the act too, and was prickling like I'd swallowed a cactus. Unfortunately, it was too soon to take more painkillers, so I'd just have to survive till I arrived home.

Before I did that, though, I needed some Leo therapy.

A nicker of welcome greeted me as I approached my horse's stable. He seemed to know there was something amiss, and stood quietly when I circled my arms around his shoulders, hugging him tight.

Warm breath tickled the back of my neck, and the comforting smell of horse soothed my soul. After only five minutes, I felt better. My head was still sore, but I was ready to face the world again. And I'd realised that I had a phone call to make.

Standing with my arm draped loosely over Leo's back, I dialled Nicholas' number. "Are you okay to speak?" I asked when he answered.

"For a minute, yes." I thought I could hear tension in his voice, perhaps because it was unheard of for me to contact him after hours.

"It's just—" in a rush, I told him about the incident at the tube station, how it *might* have been an accident, but that I was suspicious it had been deliberate.

"Where are you right now?"

"At the stables with my horse."

"Alone?"

"No, there are a few others here."

"What about when you get home?"

"I have a flatmate, she'll be back soon." And then I remembered—tonight was Trinity's hot date with Theo Yourdis the firefighter. So she probably wouldn't be in until late.

Nicholas had ploughed on, though, unaware of my inner dialogue. "All right, so tomorrow you'll work from home. I'll send Devlin over to yours with your incognito laptop. You can both dial in to the secure network and carry on your enquiries from there." There was a slight pause, then he added, obviously as an afterthought, "If that's okay with you?"

"It's fine." It would be weird to have a co-worker in my house, but I'd cope. "So I'll see him at, what, ten o'clock?"

"Maybe a little earlier. I'll phone him now and see if he can get into work a little earlier than usual."

"Right. I have to go to the stables early doors, but I'll make sure I'm home from nine onwards."

"Perfect."

"Oh—one more thing."

"Yes?" Nicholas' clipped tones told me that he'd considered our conversation ended.

"Could you ask Dev to please bring coffee?"

———

PARKING my car in its space near the door of the apartment building, I stepped out and checked nervously all around me, before hurrying to the main entrance and letting myself in.

Briefly, I considered calling on Mrs Lacey, so I wouldn't be alone in the house. But then I suddenly realised that, even if the Robin Hood hacker somehow had my address, we were in a different flat now!

Relief flooded my body. Nobody knew my new location apart from Trinity, my landlord, a few firefighters and a couple of neighbours. Certainly no-one at work would be aware I'd moved house. Dev could just find out when he pressed the buzzer to get in.

But that thought made me cautious again. I knocked at Mrs Lacey's door.

My neighbour answered quickly, wearing a lilac twinset and pearls over a tweed skirt and low-heeled shoes. She reminded me of one of my great-aunts in Scotland. "Why, Izzy, it's lovely to see you." She opened the door wider. "Come on in. I baked some scones this afternoon."

I held up a hand. "I'll not, thanks all the same. It's been a long day, and I've got a splitting headache. I just want to get home and put my feet up. But first I have a favour to ask."

"Of course, dear, of course. You know I'll always try to help you, if I can."

"It's not much. It's just—if anyone presses the entry phone and asks for me or Trinity, will you not let them in? Even if they say it's a delivery? I'll let you know if I'm expecting someone." At her quizzical look, I explained, "Trinity's ex is stirring up trouble. But nobody knows I've moved upstairs, and I want to keep it that way."

She raised her eyebrows, but, bless her, she didn't question my garbled explanation. "Anything for you, dear. Now," she held up a finger, "wait there just one minute, and I'll get you some scones to take away with you."

Before I had time to protest, she was pressing a plastic container of home baking into my hands. "You're an angel," I said.

"Don't be silly," she said, then made a flapping motion with her hand. "Now, off you get and tuck yourself up."

Raising my palm in farewell, I clambered up the stairs, desperate to get hold of some pills to rid of this headache. The tickly throat had been joined by a thick nose, symptoms that my fuddled brain eventually pieced together as potentially being a winter cold, rather than just a mere headache. I rolled my eyes. That was all I needed.

By the time Trinity arrived home a few hours later, in a cloud of happiness and Dior perfume, I was coddled on the couch with a big pack of tissues, a large mug of hot lemon and honey, and the TV playing CSI-Miami box sets.

"How was the date?" I croaked, putting my laptop onto the coffee table.

"Aw, it was lovely," she said, almost glowing with joy. "He's such a nice guy. But," her face clouded, "what's up with you?"

"I think I've caught a chill."

"Well, you should be in bed, then, Izzy, not out here getting cold."

I pointed at the electric fire, which had both bars blazing. "I'm nice and warm."

She put her hands on her hips. "Hmmm. Right, tell you what. I'll make us both a hot drink, you can tell me all about your day and *then* you get off to bed?"

"Yes, Mum," I said, then dissolved into a fit of coughing.

Her eyebrows rocketed heavenwards, but she refrained from responding to my cheeky comment. Instead, she came back a few minutes later with tea and sympathy. "So, fill me in," she said, "what's the latest on the hacker?"

I shook my head. "Nothing, sadly. Except..." in my groggy state, I'd actually forgotten about the tube platform incident. But I couldn't face explaining it all to her, it would take more energy than I could muster right now. Instead, I changed tack. "Except, Dev is coming over here to work tomorrow."

"Really?" Her eyebrows started climbing northwards again. "Is something going on between you two?"

"Nothing like that. But we think we're being spied on at the office. Hopefully, it'll be more secure here."

Trinity's eyes fell on my laptop screen. "Isn't that Veronica?"

It was my turn to raise my eyebrows at her. "Yeah. She asked me to investigate her new man. Somehow," I gave her a pointed look, "she knew about me finding things on social media."

"Ah." Trinity had the grace to blush.

"It's okay, she's paying me. And I found something out. I'll tell her tomorrow."

My friend's eyes widened. "So what did you find?"

I tapped the side of my nose. "Client-investigator privilege." The side of my mouth twitched upwards. "But she'll probably tell you if you ask."

"So you're an investigator now?"

"Seems so." As if I didn't have enough else to do...

CHAPTER TWELVE

THE NEXT MORNING, Trinity took one look at my flushed face and bloodshot eyes, and ordered me back to bed.

"But I've got Leo to ride," I protested.

"No way, Jose. I'll make sure he gets looked after for you."

I wanted to object and say that I was fine, but my body wasn't cooperating. My shoulders had an anvil pressing down on them, and my ribs were wearing a corset one size too tight. Plus, my throat was on fire and my head was full of wool. Really, I was in no fit state to go anywhere.

"Okay," I said weakly, and thirty seconds afterward I had collapsed back on my bed and into a dreamless sleep.

A persistent buzzing woke me two hours later.

"Wha—" I groped around on the bedside table for my phone.

"Izzy!" Dev's tinny voice boomed out of the speaker. "I'm outside. Let me in!"

"Urgh." I groaned something unintelligible at him, and almost turned over and went back to dreamland. But before I could do that, he squawked some more, and I forced myself to swing my legs out of bed. By some superhuman effort, I managed to stagger to the other side of the room, into my dressing gown, and out to the front door. I pressed the entry release button and said, "Top floor. Flat B."

"Oh. Okay." Dev's voice sounded even weirder on the intercom.

While he was climbing the stairs, I hurried back to my bedroom and swapped my pyjamas for jeans and a warm fleece. I was just pulling wooly socks onto my feet when the doorbell rang.

"Would you look at you!" was his greeting when I let him in.

I ran a hand through my medium-length brown hair, which was no doubt sticking out at all sorts of angles, as it hadn't seen a hairbrush since yesterday. "Sorry," I croaked. "I've got a cold."

Dev took a step back and made the sign of the cross with his fingers. "Would you believe it," he said, "I forgot my garlic."

"That's for vampires, silly." I opened the door wider and ushered him in.

"Where shall I put these?" He indicated the cardboard tray he was holding, containing two large take-away cups.

"You're a lifesaver." I pointed him at the kitchen counter. "Drop stuff on table. Put fire on. I'll brush hair. Be back one minute." Somehow, my glue-like brain could only construct short sentences. This was going to be a long day.

———

THE COFFEE DEV had brought was hot and *very* strong. So strong that it actually permeated some of the fog in my head, enough to let me work a little.

And a little was all it took.

Dev's prediction from yesterday that the personnel database would be easy to crack proved correct, and within half an hour I was looking at search results showing all of our colleagues with computer science qualifications.

"Look at this," I called him over. He peered over my shoulder, and I pointed at the list on the screen.

It contained all the usual suspects, the ones I'd been checking for days. But there was one extra name we hadn't expected:

Walter Oxley.

It seemed that Mr Oxley had obtained a First in Computer Science from Brunel University, then changed tack and done a Master's degree in Business, finishing off with an Accountancy qualification. Those later achievements were what had allowed him to climb the corporate ladder, eventually ending up as Deputy Financial Officer at one of our rival banks, and then CFO at Bleubank.

Dev sat down in the chair next to me with a thump, and we stared at each other.

"Could it be him?" I asked, not believing the answer could be so simple.

"It could well. Let me check—I'll use the Robin Hood password and his email as a username, and try to log in to that Zurich Privée Bank account."

While Dev tapped away on his computer keyboard, I pulled out the Secret Santa rhyme, and chewed my lip. The person who'd written it had known Oxo's password, and they'd obviously known something was going on.

"D'you think," I interrupted Dev, "that my Secret Santa could've been Iris, Oxley's secretary?"

He looked, up, green eyes roving around the room as he turned that over in his mind. "You might have something there. It would definitely fit. She wouldn't have the computer skills to investigate, but she'd likely realise that things were out of whack."

"I can't think of anyone else it could be." I smiled. "Hopefully that's one mystery solved. I'll try to speak to her once everything has died down." Rolling my neck, I stood and went to put the kettle on. My head was starting to thicken again, and I needed more paracetamol and cold remedy if I was to carry on working.

"Bingo!" Dev shouted as I carried two steaming drinks toward the table. Then his jaw fell open. "Would you look at that!" His index finger touched the screen. "I don't think I've ever seen that many zeroes on a bank account before. The man's minted."

My mouth fell open too, and I quickly put the mugs down, before I dropped them. "It's not his money, though," I pointed out. "He's been stealing it from Bleubank. It's no wonder the profits were down."

Dev's jaw tightened. "That's right. And with the amount those managers earn, you'd think he'd be happy, and not be trying to embezzle more. It makes me mad."

"Some people never have enough," I said, and then my mind made a little connection. "Or maybe he has an expensive ex-wife. Remember I discovered that Lee Isaacson was his stepson?"

Cogs turned in Dev's brain. "I'll bet it was Lee who tried to sabotage you." His voice rose. "Ginger-headed mongrel. Just wait till I get him." He slammed his fist onto the table, then got up and stalked round the room like a caged bear.

"Cool it, Dev," I said in as calm a tone as I could manage with a throat that felt like sandpaper. "He'll get what's due to him, and I'm fine. No harm done."

He growled. "More by good luck than anything." But his posture relaxed a little, and he thumped down into his seat again. He took a gulp of the tea I'd made him, then frowned. "So, what do we do now?"

While thoughts tried to free themselves from the treacle

that was my brain, I picked up a pen and turned it end over end. "I think all we can do is tell Nicholas," I said eventually.

"But we can't just leave the money there. He might move it again."

"We need it as evidence. Otherwise he could just deny everything."

"We could take screenshots?"

I fiddled with the pen some more, thinking. "Okay, how's about you do the screenshots, then we'll make a new, secure account at Bleubank and move all his money into that. *Then* we tell Nicholas and let him inform the police and the board of directors."

His face brightened. "I could live with that. Let's make it so!"

I grinned. "You're such a nerd!"

———

HALF-WAY THROUGH THE AFTERNOON, Dev and I had moved more money that either of us was ever likely to see again, Nicholas was cock-a-hoop that we'd solved the mystery, and my body had decided that it'd done more than enough for one day.

"I need to get back to bed," I groaned.

"But it's the karaoke tonight. You've got to come!"

My watch said it was only three thirty. Trinity was seeing Theo the firefighter again tonight, so I'd be on my own in the flat. But I really was *not* feeling sociable.

"I couldn't face the journey into town, Dev, if I'm honest. My body feels like I've run ten marathons back-to-back. I need some sleep. Plus, I'll just infect everyone else with my cold." I grimaced. "You've probably got it already."

He made a face. "So, if I've got it already, I'll pass it on to everyone else tonight, anyway."

There was some logic in that.

"I have an idea." Raising a hand, he cast his eyes around the room. "Do you have a DVD player?"

"Uh, yes." I pointed at a silver box on a shelf underneath the telly.

His expression lit up. "How about *we* take the karaoke to *you*?"

My brain couldn't make sense of that. "What? How?"

"I'll get the gang to come round here," he must've seen the look on my face, because he added, "in a few hours, once you've had some sleep. We'll bring some beers and a carry-out, play karaoke on a DVD, then leave you to get your beauty sleep by ten o'clock. How's that sound?"

I stared around the room, wondering if I had enough energy to do housework. But then I realised that, since we'd just moved, and half my stuff was still downstairs, the place was actually pretty clean and tidy.

"Okay. As long as you won't be offended if I have to take myself off to bed before the evening's over."

He held up a hand, three fingers pointing in the air. "Scout's honour."

"Another condition. Make sure Charlie Thwaite gets asked along. But *don't*, under any circumstances, invite Lee, or let him get wind of it or find out where I live. I don't want my flat torched."

"Right. Need-to-know basis only. I can do that. I'll head off now and start organising things."

———

A couple of hours sleep and an invigorating shower seemed to be sufficient to revive me enough to enjoy the party. And I used my dodgy throat as an excuse not to sing, which was a kindness to everyone else, given how tone-deaf I was.

We were half-way through the evening, and even Nicholas was starting to loosen up, when the door of the flat opened and Trinity walked in, her face pale. With a frown, she looked around the room, obviously not understanding what was going on. "Have I got the wrong place?" she asked.

I hurried over. "Long story," I said, "it's my workmates. Since I wasn't well, they decided to bring the night out to me." I jerked my chin back. "Are *you* okay? You don't look right."

"I—" she shook her head. "I'll tell you in the morning." Her eyes lit up. "Is that roasted peanuts over there?"

"Yeah. Come and join the party." I ushered her into the throng. "Everyone, this is Trinity, my flatmate." I started telling her everyone's names, but she stopped me with a laugh.

"I'll forget," she said. "I'll just call you all Bleu One, or Bleu Two or whatever. Okay?"

In a corner, Dev was deep in conversation with Charlie, oblivious to all that was going on around about. I smiled. Maybe this impromptu event would have an unexpectedly good outcome.

CHAPTER THIRTEEN

On Monday, Dev came round to my apartment again, and we spent the day watching vintage Star Trek episodes and drinking cold remedy. It felt decadent, but we'd agreed with Nicholas on Friday afternoon that it would be politic for us to keep out of the office until the repercussions of our discovery had died down.

Officially, we were both on sick days—which was true anyway, since Dev now had man flu and was practically dead on his feet, and I still hadn't recovered from my cold.

Staying at home also made me feel safer, as we weren't sure if the board had done anything about Oxo and Lee on Friday, or whether they'd wait till things opened up on Monday before telling the police. Either way, we should both be clear to go back into the office the next day.

When I woke up on Tuesday, my cold had subsided enough that my brain was feeling more normal, although my lungs were still clogged and I was coughing a hundred times per hour.

Nicholas had ordered me to take a taxi in, and charge it to

the firm's account, so I arrived in style. It was a luxury I knew I shouldn't get used to, but I figured I perhaps deserved it.

After all, between us, Dev and I had solved the mystery of the anomalous data, and, in the process, had discovered lost revenues that would bolster the bank's profits and keep the shareholders happy.

I'd made the driver take a detour via the coffee shop, so I was clutching my re-usable cup when I entered the office. Things seemed strangely subdued. Or was it me? Was I expecting some kind of fanfare or celebration, like a victorious hunter returned to camp? I laughed at myself. We British didn't *do* things like that.

Reaching my desk, I said 'hello' to my colleagues, switched on my computer, then groaned at the sight of my Inbox. It would take me most of the morning to sort that out.

Squaring my shoulders, I took a slug of coffee, and applied myself to my emails.

Dev arrived a short time later, looking pleased with himself. He reached over the partition and gave me a high five, before disappearing behind his computer monitor. I assumed that he, too, was fighting his way through an ocean of emails. I didn't expect to see him this side of Christmas.

When my eyes were starting to cross from the amount of junk in my email folders, I decided it was time for a change.

There was one more thread of the mystery that I needed to tie up.

In deference to my struggling lungs, I took the lift to the top floor. Plush carpet absorbed every footfall and framed artworks hung on the walls like trophies. It was a different world up here. Even the air seemed rarified.

Near the end of the corridor, I knocked on a solid mahogany door. "Come in," called a thin voice.

Behind her desk in the reception area before the CFO's office, Iris Hooper flushed bright red at the sight of me. I didn't need to say a word to know that she was my Secret Santa. It was written all over her face.

"You found out," she said tremulously, a small hand patting nervously at her grey curls.

"Yes, thanks to you." I smiled reassuringly. "But if you hadn't given me the Robin Hood connection, I might never have solved the mystery."

"Silly man," she shook her head, silver earrings twinkling as she did so. "He thought he was so clever, yet he used the same password for everything."

My forehead scrunched. "What was the fourteen fifty-four thing?"

"His birthday," she said simply. "One, four, fifty-four."

"Oh! I thought it was something to do with Robin Hood." I pointed at the inner sanctum behind her. "He's gone, I assume?"

Her chin lifted. "Yesterday."

"Well, thanks for the clues," I said, "and thanks for the voucher. I'll use it to get some new riding gloves." I smiled at her. "I'll not keep you any longer."

I'd got as far as the door when one further errant thread popped into my brain. "Oh, another thing—was it you that told the 404 hacker group?"

She pressed her lips together. "You mustn't tell, but my nephew is a member. At first, I thought he would be able to work out what Mr Oxley was doing, but the security here was just too good for the hackers to crack it."

That made my heart glow. I'd have to tell the others that what we were doing was making a difference.

"So then I tried you," she continued, "You seemed like an honest, clever girl. I was sure you'd decipher it."

"It was lucky you got me as your Secret Santa, then."

Stifling a smile, she waved a well-manicured finger at her computer. "Not so lucky, really. It's me that organises the list!"

———

AT LUNCHTIME I popped my head round the corner and attracted Dev's attention. "Lunch?" I asked. "Sandwich at the church?"

"Could do." Then his cheeks coloured. "Er, would it be okay if Charlie joined us?"

I grinned. Looked like Charlie had got her man. "Of course."

———

TUESDAY AFTER WORK was the first time I'd felt well enough to ride Leo in days.

My lung capacity was still abysmal, so I had to keep it simple, but it was just great to be back aboard my boy again. The partnership we had was so special to me, and when he was going well, it truly felt like we were dancing together.

Trinity had been doing the majority of the cooking since the weekend, although I'd not had much of an appetite, so mostly I'd been eating soup or toast. But on Tuesday night, she had promised to produce another of her tasty Caribbean dishes.

I walked through the door of the flat, nostrils flaring at the amazing scents wafting toward me, glanced at the kitchen, then stopped in surprise. "Trinity! Your hair!" Stepping closer, I turned a circle around her to get a better look.

Gone were her long dark tresses, and in their place was a stylish pixie cut that made her look like a younger version of Halle Berry. "Wow!" I said. "I love it." I wrinkled my brow. "But what inspired you to get it all cut off?"

She spooned food onto two plates and angled her head at the table. "Sit yourself down and I'll tell you."

Over another delicious meal, she explained. "I never told you, did I, about Friday night?"

"Friday?" I felt like I was missing something. "At the karaoke?"

"No. Before that. Remember—I was out with Theo."

"Oh, of course! I was so bunged up with the cold I forgot. Sorry." I frowned. "You came home early, didn't you?"

"Yeah." Her eyes narrowed. "I walked out on 'im." She took another mouthful of food, then carried on with her story.

"We went to the pub, and then when I asked for a second Prosecco, he refused. Said that I'd had enough, that I'd end up making a spectacle of myself if I had too much to drink. I ask you," she lifted a hand in the air, "how long had 'e known me? About three days. And had 'e ever seen me drunk? No. Me, I don't *get* drunk. I know when to stop. And besides which," she gave a wry smile, "I can't afford it."

"So what happened then?"

"Well, next thing 'e was criticising my clothes, telling me that my skirt was too short and that I'd be giving other men the wrong impression. Do you know what I did then?"

I shook my head.

"I stood up," her cheeks flushed as she remembered the altercation, "slapped his face, and stormed out of the pub, straight into a taxi, and back here."

"Oh, wow. No wonder you seemed upset. I'm sorry I forgot to ask you on Saturday."

"Don't you worry. You weren't well. And I were hardly here."

I felt a bit guilty at that. Trinity had looked after Leo for me at the weekend, free of charge.

"So, I decided, I've 'ad enough of men. I'm going it alone. I'm not 'aving anyone control me." She ran a hand through her trendy, short hair. "An' this is like me saying to the world, I'm a new woman."

I fingered a lock of my own shoulder-length hair, wondering if I should follow her lead and get mine cut off too. But I didn't want to seem like a copy-cat.

"How shall we celebrate?" I asked. "I got some more ice-cream."

"And CSI?"

"Perfect!"

CHAPTER FOURTEEN

On Wednesday evening, I turned up at the Community Centre for my Pilates class and found a throng of people crowding around the door, talking nineteen to the dozen. Spotting the tall figure of Queenie at the front, I pushed my way through. "What's going on?" I asked.

In answer, she pointed at a poster stuck to the glass. 'Closed until further notice', it declared.

"The plumbing finally gave out," she said, "and the council hasn't got any money to fix it."

"So the class is off?"

"I'm afraid so. Until I can find us somewhere else, anyway."

"Let me know. Thanks. And Merry Christmas!"

"You too," she replied, but I could tell her mind was elsewhere.

It was still early evening, but I'd ridden Leo in the morning—as best I could, with my lungs only working at fifty percent capacity—so there didn't seem to be anything left to do except go home.

When I walked through the apartment door a short while

later, I discovered Trinity sitting at the kitchen table, her head in her hands.

"What am I going to do?" she moaned.

I blinked at her for a minute, then light dawned. "Are your classes off too?"

She nodded. "All I've got left are a couple of measly Salsa sessions in Wimbledon. Everything else were at the community centre here in Putney. The stables don't pay me much. How will I ever afford the rent?" She went back to staring at the table.

I put a hand on her shoulder. "Don't worry about it for now. The rent's covered, remember? And Queenie said she was going to find somewhere else to run Pilates. Maybe you can find another place too."

With a sigh, I slumped down on the couch. Things had been going so well. But now my friend was in trouble, and it was affecting me too. With a start, I realised, for the first time, that I really *liked* having her stay here. In fact, I preferred it to being on my own.

That was quite a revelation to me.

I'd always seen myself as an animal person, not a people person. And yet, here I was, worrying about losing my flatmate, and trying to work out if there was anything I could do to help her.

They said that people didn't change. But they were obviously wrong.

———

It was Thursday morning before I saw Veronica again, to give her the results of my investigations.

"Veronica," I said, leaning over her stable door, "I haven't seen you all week, but I wanted to tell you what I'd found out in person, rather than on the phone."

She finished wrapping an exercise bandage around her horse's leg, then stood up. "My dear, that's just wonderful. I never expected you to find anything out so quickly."

I refrained from telling her that it had only taken me a little over an hour last Thursday evening, and that pretty much anyone who could use FaceBook or Google could have found out the same information. "I'm afraid it's not the best news," I said, concerned that her expectations would be dashed.

"Is that so?" She shook her head. "Why is it I'm not surprised?" Leaning against her horse's side, she gazed intently at me. "Tell me everything."

A short while later, I was two hundred pounds better off —"You've saved me more than that in heartache, darlin', I can't thank you enough"—and Veronica had discovered that Kenneth Yates, alternatively known as Ken the Pen, was a skilled con man with a long history of fleecing rich women.

With a feeling of satisfaction, I turned to my own horse. Maybe I could get him that new bridle after all.

But, with only two days to go before the final of the Parkside League, I was getting a bit twitchy about how little riding I was able to do. By the time I'd groomed him and tacked him up, I had limited energy left to ride. It seemed like this cold would never go away.

"Coo-ee!" Suzie popped her head over the door just as I was struggling with Leo's girth.

"Oh, hi Suzie. Are you on a back shift today?"

"Yes, I did a swap with someone else." She frowned at me. "Are you having some difficulty there?"

"It's just this cold. It's wiped me out. Even the simplest jobs are an effort."

"Aw, that's not good. Are you managing to ride?"

"Barely. I'm going to try again now. I need to practise for the dressage on Saturday."

"Oooh, of course. I remember you said you was going to that. I'll let you get on, then."

"Thanks." I led Leo out of the stable and went off to the arena.

Thirty minutes later I was back, feeling like a wet dishrag. I'd done more than I had for a while, and it had wiped me out.

Suzie took one look at my face and grabbed Leo's reins off me. "I'll untack him for you. You sit yourself down, love, get your breath back."

I didn't have the energy to argue with her. Sitting on an upturned bucket, I put my elbows on my knees and my chin in my hands, waiting until my head stopped spinning.

It seemed like only moments afterward that a bright voice said above me, "I'll just take him out to the field for you." It was Trinity.

"Are you sure?"

Suzie appeared at that point with a mug of sweet tea. "Drink this," she instructed, "I think you need it."

Twenty minutes later, after the ministrations of my two friends, I was feeling a lot better, and ready to face a day at work. Before I left, they sat me down.

"Firstly," said Trinity, "you've to get a taxi to the station today. Okay?"

Pursing my lips, I remembered the two hundred pounds in my pocket. I supposed I could afford it. "Okay," I agreed.

"Secondly," this time it was Suzie, "Trinity and I have made a plan. We'll be your grooms for Saturday, for the competition. We'll do your horse, so all you'll have to worry about is riding."

"But I thought you were on night shift at the weekend?"

"I'll swap shifts again so I can be there. We want you to do yourself justice. And that'll not happen if you're still unwell and having to do everything on your own."

Tears pricked my eyes. "Are you sure?"

"We're sure," said Susie.

Trinity nodded her agreement. "Team Leo is behind you."

I had to fight hard not to cry. "Thanks. You guys are the best." It would be lovely, for a change, to be at a competition with friends, rather than on my own. What was it they said? Teamwork makes the dream work? I hoped they were correct.

Now all I had to do was manage to ride for longer than half an hour on Saturday without collapsing. I could do that, couldn't I?

———

I'D ONLY JUST ARRIVED at the office that morning when Dev and Nicholas came striding toward our team's section. Dev had a spring in his step and a smile on his face. He stopped at my desk and asked, "Audi or BMW, Izzy, what d'you think?"

Taken aback, my forehead puckered. But before I had time to ask him to explain himself, Nicholas called me over. "Join me in meeting room two," he said, and marched off. Dev gave me a thumbs up.

Running a hand through my hair, I stared after our team leader. Then, with a shake of my head, I grabbed my coffee and followed him out of the office. Nothing was making much sense this morning.

Five minutes later, I understood why Dev had looked so happy.

Bleubank executive, Nicholas explained, were so pleased with the outcome of our investigations, that they were going to increase our bonuses. He named a five-figure sum. A significant amount of money, almost life-changing. I gulped.

But I wasn't to brag about it, Nicholas cautioned, because Dev and I were the only ones whose bonuses had increased.

"In return," Nicholas continued, "they have asked that you sign this non-disclosure agreement." He pushed a sheaf of papers across the table at me. "We don't want anyone else to realise how easy it was to subvert our systems."

"But, I'd never tell a soul," I protested. "Why would I?"

Nicholas shrugged his thin shoulders. "I believe you. But I know you. The board don't. It's merely... extra insurance on their part. You understand?"

Pulling my coffee towards me, I took a mouthful. I needed time to think, and I needed caffeine to lubricate my brain.

"Let me just have a read." I picked up the paperwork and began to scan the paragraphs of text. But it was all in corporate jargon and legalese, and difficult for a lay person to decipher.

As much as I could understand, it was exactly as Nicholas had said. They were asking that I never disclose any details of the fraud perpetrated by 'a member of senior staff'. That seemed to be it.

"Okay," I said, and signed at the bottom. Twice, since there was a copy for me, and one for the company.

Nicholas also signed, as witness. "That's that then," he said, putting the cap back on his pen. "The money will be in your account by Christmas. Good work."

And that was it. Just like that, I was tens of thousands of pounds richer.

———

IT WAS ABOUT two o'clock when Dev and I returned from a celebratory lunch. He'd decided on an Audi; I'd decided to buy a young horse to train on, and maybe a lorry to take me to competitions as well. Or a deposit on a flat. I needed to think about that one.

Passing through reception on our way back to the office, we noticed all the smartly-dressed people heading up the stairs. Dev tilted his head. "Must be the shareholder meeting."

"Oh, that's right, it was today, wasn't it?" Spotting a pile of glossy brochures on the reception desk, I picked one up and leafed through it idly as we climbed the stairs. Dev had opened the door to our floor and was holding it for me when I stopped dead. "The toe rags!" I exclaimed. "The scumbags! The total shysters!"

Dev shut the door again and looked furtively around. "What's up?"

I held out the brochure—Bleubank's Annual Report—and jabbed my finger at a section of text.

Reaching for it, Dev read the paragraph, and his jaw fell open. "They're taking the Mick, aren't they?"

"Nope. This is the annual report, Dev. It's there for the whole world to see."

"The ratbags! That NDA they got us to sign, that was—"

I put my hand up, suddenly aware of how our voices were echoing in the concrete and metal stairwell. "Let's take it outside," I said, feeling not a single shred of guilt at extending our lunch hour. I think I'd subconsciously realised I was going to leave. I just hadn't verbalised it yet.

A few minutes later, we were sitting under the oak tree by the old church once more. Dev had calmed down slightly, but he was still fuming. "So that NDA was to stop us telling the police. I can't believe they let that crook away with it. And with a golden handshake as well!" He looked me in the eye. "Especially since he tried to kill you."

"I've been thinking about that. I think it was perhaps Lee that went after me. Remember they were plotting in the coffee shop. But have you noticed Lee's not around any more?"

"That's as maybe. It was still Oxo who put him up to it."

I sighed. "You're probably right."

He got up off the bench and stomped about. "Why would they do that? Why would they let such a cheating criminal walk away scot-free?"

Crossing my legs, I wrapped my arms around my knees and rested my chin while I thought. "It's all about the shareholders," I realised, thinking out loud. "They don't want to admit to being defrauded, they don't want to admit to the poor judgement that elected him onto the board, and they don't want to admit how close they came to insolvency."

"So, it's all about saving face?" Dev had stopped his pacing and faced me, his hands on his hips.

"Looks like it."

He growled. "That's it, I've absolutely had enough. As soon as that money hits my bank account, I'm done. I'm handing in my notice. PayPal or no PayPal. I'll find something else, so I will."

I gazed at the concrete jungle around us. This peaceful church with its ancient tree was like an oasis of calm in a crazy city. But I was sick and tired of the rat race. "I'm getting out too."

"What will you do? Dublin?" He looked hopeful for a moment. Maybe Charlie hadn't totally bewitched him. I felt sad for her.

"Nope. I don't know exactly what yet, but I've had it up to here with cities. I want to live in the country again. Somewhere everybody knows your name."

CHAPTER FIFTEEN

IT WAS Saturday before the answer came to me.

I'd survived my two dressage tests, and my gorgeous Leo had behaved impeccably. While we waited for the results to be announced, I was once more sitting on an upturned bucket, and Team Leo were doing their thing around me, sponging my horse down and preparing him to travel back to the stables.

Suzie had given me a copy of Horse & Hound magazine to read while I waited. I was scanning the classifieds, wondering if anyone had a nice youngster for sale, when a block advert caught my attention.

My eyes widened and I rocked back, almost tipping the bucket over in my excitement.

But before I could say anything, the tannoy crackled and a voice boomed, "Could all the prizewinners in the Parkside League please come to the main arena for the prize-giving. In first place, Miss Isobel Paterson and her horse Leo—"

I didn't hear any more, for Suzie and Trinity pulled me up and danced us round in some kind of demented polka, screaming and laughing and crying all at the same time.

My insides felt all fuzzy. Teamwork really *had* made the dream work!

When they finally calmed down enough for me to speak, I clutched Trinity's shoulder. "Look at this." I pointed at the advert, then handed the magazine over. "D'you fancy it?"

Wanted: *Horse trainer*

To work with young horses using Natural Horsemanship methods.

Live-in position. Small salary. Own horse welcome.

Would possibly suit couple as groom's position also vacant.

Apply to Lady Alice Letham, Glengowrie Stud, Perthshire.

She read the text, then looked up at me, her face shining. "You think there's much call for Salsa classes up there?"

I grinned. "Why don't we write to her and find out?"

———

THE END

———

Want to read more *about Izzy and Trinity, and the mysteries they encounter in the Highlands of Scotland?*

Order the next book, ***A Corpse at the Castle***:

Read on for a sample:

AN EXCERPT FROM A CORPSE AT THE CASTLE

DINNER LONG FINISHED—A tasty mushroom risotto followed by raspberry cranachan—Craig and I had got to the part of the evening when you reminisce about TV programmes you watched as a child, arguing about who was the best character and who had the most memorable catchphrase.

We were busy discussing the Blue Peter pets—they were much more important than the presenters, naturally—when the outside door opened with a gust of wind and a trim old lady stepped carefully over the threshold. Wearing a tweed skirt and cashmere jumper, she had white-grey hair permed in loose waves round her head.

For a moment I thought the Queen had come to visit.

Beside me, Craig straightened in his seat. Maybe he was thinking the same thing.

The old lady's nostrils flared as if scenting for prey, and her sharp eyes darted from left to right, scanning the room. When she spotted Craig, she hurried over. "Mr MacDonald," she said in a breathy voice, "have you seen my Hamish here this evening?"

Not the Queen, then. I was a little disappointed. It would have been a good story. And it would've been nice to know that royalty could escape protocol now and again and have a drink in a pub like the rest of us. *Poor woman.* I'd realised long ago that having lots of money wasn't all it was cracked up to be.

Craig shook his head. "I'm sorry, Mrs Douglas, he's no' been in th'night." It seemed like a few beers made Craig's accent stronger.

Hamish's wife turned her mouth down and thrust her hands onto her hips, scanning the bar again. "Where can he be?" she said, almost to herself.

"He was at the stables this afternoon," I offered. "I left him in his office."

Head tilting like a sparrow who's spotted a stray crumb, her bright eyes focussed on me. "And you are...?"

"Izzy Paterson." I held out a hand. "I work for Lady Letham. Brought a couple of mares up to stud earlier."

"Nice to meet you," she said perfunctorily, but her mind was obviously elsewhere.

"Could it be that a client brought him a bottle o' whisky, and he's in his office doing a quality check?" Craig offered, slowly spinning his empty beer bottle, rotating it on its thick base. He gave me a quick glance.

She pressed her lips together and clenched a fist. "Maybe. I'd better go check." Without a backward glance she was off, leaving the pub door swinging wildly behind her.

I raised my eyebrows at her departure, then nodded at Craig's empty bottle. "Is it my round?"

He shook his head. "I'd better call it a night. I've an early start wi' the garrons the morn." He speared me with those green eyes. "Can I walk you back to the B&B?"

My stomach flipped. "I—It's okay," I stammered, suddenly tongue-tied. Somehow, with the arrival of Mrs Douglas, the atmosphere had shifted. "There's no need. I can't imagine there's any Jack the Rippers in a wee place like this."

He lifted a shoulder. "It'll be no trouble. It's on my way home."

Want to find out what happens next?
Get the next book, ***A Corpse at the Castle***:

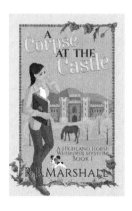

A NOTE FROM THE AUTHOR

Thank you for reading, and I really hope you enjoyed the story. If so, please take a moment to leave a review and tell a friend!

THE HIGHLAND HORSE WHISPERER SERIES

Sign up to my newsletter to be the first to find out about special offers, and when the next book will be available:

rozmarshall.co.uk/newsletter,

or find the series—and my other books—at:

rozmarshall.co.uk/books.

ALSO BY R.B. MARSHALL

The **Highland Horse Whisperer** series

Cozy Mystery set in Scotland (and London for the prequel):

- *The Secret Santa Mystery*
- *A Corpse at the Castle*
- *A Right Royal Revenge*
- *A Henchman at the Highland Games* (due in 2021)

WRITING AS ROZ MARSHALL:

The **Celtic Fey** series

Urban Fantasy / Young Adult Fantasy set in Scotland (and the faerie realm):

- *Kelpie Curse*
- *Faerie Quest*
- *The Fey Bard*
- *Merlin's Army* (due early 2021)

Secrets in the Snow series

Women's Fiction / Sweet Sports Romance set in a Scottish ski school:

- *Fear of Falling*
- *My Snowy Valentine*
- *The Racer Trials*
- *Snow Blind*
- *Weathering the Storm*

Half Way Home *stories*

Young Adult Science Fiction set in Hugh Howey's *Half Way Home* universe:

- *Nobody's Hero*
- *The Final Solution*

Scottish stories*:*

- *Still Waters*

WRITING AS BELLE MCINNES:

Mary's Ladies *series [complete]*

Scottish Historical Romance telling the story of Mary Queen of Scots:

- *A Love Divided*
- *A Love Beyond*
- *A Love Concealed*

The Macrae Legends *series*

Clean Scottish Historical Romance telling of the beginnings of Clan Macrae, during the time of William Wallace and Robert the Bruce:

- *For Love or Justice (releasing 31 Aug 2021)*

ABOUT THE AUTHOR

Like my amateur sleuth, Izzy, I'm a Scottish, dressage riding, computer geek who loves coffee—but there the similarity ends. She is far smarter than me, and a lot younger!

I hope you'll join me in discovering where her curiosity leads to next...

Get the next book: ***A Corpse at the Castle***

I ALSO WRITE IN OTHER GENRES:

Fantasy and clean romance/women's fiction, as Roz Marshall: rozmarshall.co.uk/books

Historical Romance, telling the story of Mary Queen of Scots, as Belle McInnes: books2read.com/rl/MarysLadies

Here's where you'll find me:
rozmarshall.co.uk/books

facebook.com/rozmarshallauthor

GLOSSARY

Auld Nick (Old Nick): A (Scottish) nickname for Satan
Beanie: A close-fitting hat, usually made of wool or fleece
Brass neck: Behaviour where someone is extremely confident about their own actions but doesn't understand that their behaviour is unacceptable to others
CEO: Chief Executive Officer. The top boss in a company or organisation
CFO: Chief Financial Officer. The most senior manager in charge of company finances
Cybersecurity: Protecting against the criminal or unauthorised use of electronic data, or the measures taken to achieve this
Daffodil: A yellow garden flower, associated with Easter
Dark web: A part of the **deep web**, consisting of secret networks that can only be accessed using special software or specific authorisation
Data: Information processed, transmitted or stored by a computer. It may be in the form of text documents, images, audio clips, software programs, web pages, etc
Deep web: A part of the internet containing websites or

apps which cannot be found by regular search engines such as Google

Dosh: Money

Dressage: The training and gymnasticising of horses. Also used to describe the competitions where the results of that training are demonstrated

Early doors: Early, early on

Encryption: Translating text or data by way of a secret keyword or cipher, converting it to something un-readable unless you have the cipher

Fiver: Five pounds (GBP) money

Flat: When referring to housing, an apartment. A set of rooms on a single floor, used as a dwelling.

(Painting the) Forth Rail Bridge: A never-ending task (the Forth Rail Bridge is so large and long that as soon as they get to one end, the painters have to start all over again at the other end)

Guinness: Irish beer. Dark, almost black

Hacker: a person who uses computers and computer networks to gain unauthorised access to other people's systems or data

Hashtag: a word or phrase preceded by a hash sign (#), used on social media websites and applications, especially Twitter, to identify messages on a specific topic

Horsemanship: The training of horses using 'natural' methods such as body language. Sometimes called 'Natural Horsemanship'

Horse Whisperer: A horse trainer who is adept at communicating with horses

IT: Information Technology

Janitor: Caretaker, custodian

Jobsworth: Someone who sticks to the rules. "It's more than my job's worth to do that…"

Karaoke: Interactive entertainment in which an amateur

singer sings along with recorded music (usually an instru-
mental version of a well-known popular song) using a
microphone

Keep cup: A reusable coffee cup

League (sporting): A series of sporting events where
results are awarded cumulative points, with the overall
winner being the person or team who has accumulated the
most points.

Livery Yard: A boarding facility for horses, usually with
stables and paddocks plus riding arena(s). Sometimes part of a
farm, or sometimes purpose-built. Abbreviated to '**Yard**'.

(That were) Mint: (dialect) That was good

Mobile Phone: Cellphone

Natural Horsemanship: See **Horsemanship**

NDA: Non-Disclosure Agreement

Network: The connections between computers that let
them share information or resources (such as printers). Effectively the wires between them.

Nobble: To disable, or to prevent someone (or something)
from winning

Norfolk Broads: A flat, marshy area in the English county
of Norfolk

PC: Personal computer

PI: Private Investigator

(On the) QT: On the quiet

(Lose the) rag: Get angry

RSPCA: Royal Society for the Prevention of Cruelty to
Animals

Rug: Horse blanket used to keep them warm and dry in
inclement weather

Stable: The stall or loose box where a horse is housed (if
necessary).

Stables: Either a row of individual stables, or sometimes the
whole establishment—see **Livery Yard**.

Tack: Horse equipment, usually the leatherwork such as saddle and bridle

Tights: Panty-hose, nylons

Torch: Flashlight

Trousers: Leg-wear. Pants. In the UK, pants are underpants. Here, being "caught with your pants down" has even more graphic connotations.

Tube: In the context of travel, the subway or metro system. See **Underground**

Tube train: Vehicles that run on the subway system

Two shakes (of a lamb's tail): Quickly

Underground: The subway system (in London). See **Tube**

Web browser: An application, such as Google Chrome, Firefox or Microsoft Edge, used to access information contained in websites on the world-wide-web

Wick (on my wick): Annoying

Wiggle (get a wiggle on): Hurry up

Winkle (winkle something out):

World-wide-web: Websites on the internet, connected by links (hyperlinks) and searchable by search engines such as Google

Yard: See **Livery Yard**.

Y2K: Year 2000. Many computer programs written before the millennium assumed that dates would all start with '19', and that the programs would be defunct before long. But much of that old technology was still being used in 1999, so the software had to be re-written to cope with the next century. It was known as the Y2K bug, or the Y2K problem.

CHARACTERS

Isobel (Izzy) Paterson: Computer Security Analyst working in London for Bleubank

Antoine Lanier: Bluebank employee from the Paris office
Bashir Noorzai: Izzy's landlord
Charlie Thwaite: Computer Support team member
Dwayne Brooks: Trinity's ex-boyfriend
Devlin (Dev) Connolly: Computer Security Analyst. Izzy's colleague and friend
Emma: Horse owner at the same stables as Izzy
Eric: Janitor at the community centre
Frank Varley: Computer Support team member
Gordon Dempsey (Dempo): CEO of Bleubank
Harry McPhail: Bleubank security guard
Iris Hooper: CFO's secretary
Jasmin Freeman: Dwayne's friend
Kenneth Yates: Veronica's love interest
Kirsty: Horse owner at the same stables as Izzy
Mrs Lacey: Widow in the flat downstairs to Izzy
Lee Isaacson: Computer Support team member

Leo: Izzy's dressage horse

Manda Kumar: Computer Security Analyst. Izzy's colleague

Nicholas Spence: Team leader and Izzy's boss

Pamela Emerson: Head of Computer Support

Queenie: Pilates teacher

Rob Gosling: Member of the network team

Suzannah (Suzie) Wilks: Horse owner in the next stable to Izzy

Theo Yourdis: Firefighter

Trinity Allen: Izzy's friend. Part-time groom, part-time dance teacher

Veronica Rothwell: Horse owner in the opposite stable to Izzy

Walter Oxley (Oxo): Chief Financial Officer of Bleubank

RECIPE 1 - CAPRESE PANINI
CAPRESE PANINI WITH AVOCADO BASIL PESTO

If you don't have a grill pan or a panini press, any regular skillet will get you a caprese grilled cheese that'll taste wonderful, just minus the grill marks.

Find the recipe here (scroll to the bottom of the page):

- https://www.aberdeenskitchen.com/2018/06/caprese-panini-avocado-basil-pesto/

RECIPE 2 - JAMAICAN CURRY

JAMAICAN BLACK-EYED PEA CURRY

This Jamaican black-eyed pea curry is so delicious. It's creamy, bursting with flavor, hearty, healthy and super easy to make. It's naturally gluten free and vegan. A must make recipe!

Find the recipe here:

- https://www.thecuriouschickpea.com/jamaican-black-eyed-pea-curry/

ACKNOWLEDGMENTS

Thank you to Liz, Stacy, Jen and Tonya, my beta-reading and editing team, and to the members of my critique group, Secondary Characters, who added extra polish and value to my scribblings. Much appreciated!

Made in the USA
Columbia, SC
09 November 2021

48663706R00100